THE GUARDIANS *of* GA'HOOLE

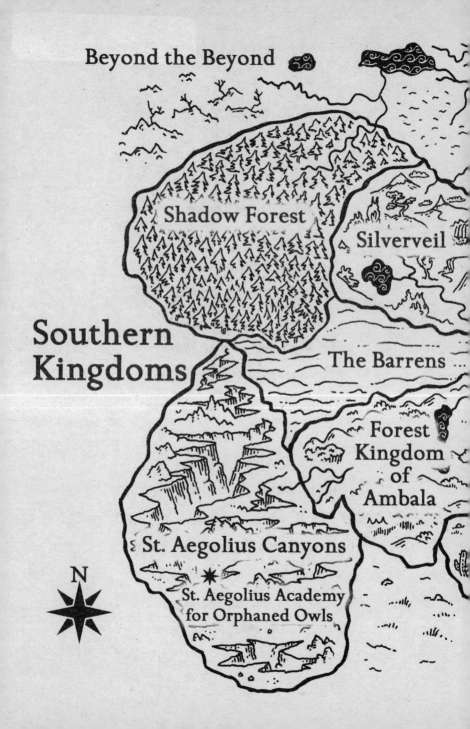

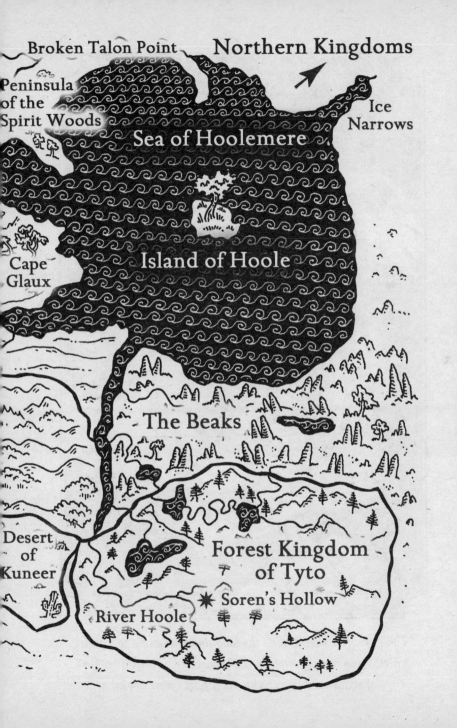

Their progress was slow as the load that Otulissa and Fritha
carried was a heavy one. In the talons of each was a botkin
of scrolls and strapped to their backs were books.

GUARDIANS
of GA'HOOLE

BOOK FOURTEEN

Exile

BY KATHRYN LASKY

SCHOLASTIC INC.

New York Toronto London Auckland
Sydney Mexico City New Delhi Hong Kong

The author is indebted to Ray Bradbury for his Fahrenheit 451 and his brilliant depiction of a society in which book burning was the norm and intellectual freedom destroyed.

No part of this publication may be reproduced, or stored in a retrieval system, or transmitted in any form or by any means, electronic, mechanical, photocopying, recording, or otherwise, without written permission of the publisher. For information regarding permission, write to Scholastic Inc., Attention: Permissions Department, 557 Broadway, New York, NY 10012.

ISBN 978-0-439-88808-0

Text copyright © 2008 by Kathryn Lasky.

Illustrations copyright © 2008 by Scholastic Inc. All rights reserved. Published by Scholastic Inc. SCHOLASTIC and associated logos are trademarks and/or registered trademarks of Scholastic Inc.

Artwork by Richard Cowdrey
Design by Steve Scott

12 11   12 13 14 15/0

Printed in the U.S.A.   40

First printing, February 2008

Northern Kingdoms

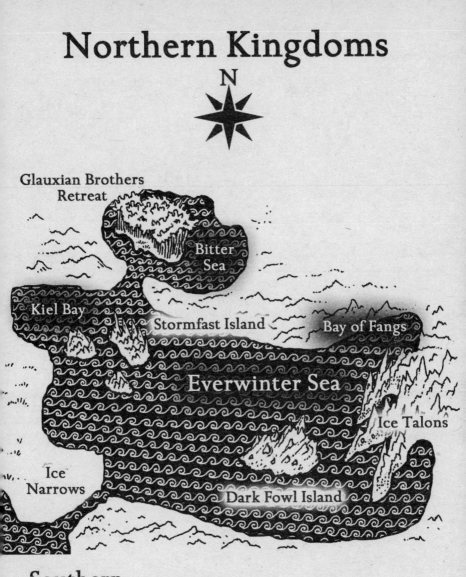

Glauxian Brothers
Retreat

Bitter
Sea

Kiel Bay

Stormfast Island

Bay of Fangs

Everwinter Sea

Ice Talons

Ice
Narrows

Dark Fowl Island

Southern
Kingdoms

GUARDIANS
of GA'HOOLE

Exile

Contents

Prologue

"All right, Otulissa, how does this sound for the lead article?" Fritha, a very diligent Pygmy Owl and one of Otulissa's best students, had become the assistant editor of The Evening Hoot, a newspaper that she and Otulissa had started shortly after Coryn came to the tree. Otulissa looked up from what she was reading.

"Yes, I'm listening."

"'The three-day Harvest Festival, one of the merriest of the great tree's many festivals, is expected to be somewhat subdued this year in deference to the blue owl, the Striga, from the newly discovered Middle Kingdom, who was so instrumental in the rescue of Bell, one of the three B's, daughter of Soren and Pelli. The Striga was also crucial in the thwarting of the heinous slink melf by the Pure Ones and their plan to assassinate our king and the Band. There will be no music or singing. Many here at the tree were looking forward to Blythe's debut with an air composed by one of the new gadfeathers that have become so numerous in our kingdoms of late. In addition to these changes in our usual celebration there will be no brewing of milkberries.'" Fritha paused. "How is it so far?"

"Depressing," Otulissa replied.

CHAPTER ONE

A Reduced Harvest Festival

But, Bell, I don't understand. I've been practicing all summer with Madame Plonk for the Milkberry Harvest Festival and now you say I shouldn't sing? I just don't understand. She'll think I don't care."

"But you shouldn't care, Blythe," Bell protested.

"Why shouldn't I care? I've worked hard on this."

"Singing is — you know — sort of prideful." Bell squirmed a bit as she said this.

"Prideful?" Blythe blinked her huge, shining black eyes.

"Yes. It's, you know, a vanity."

Blythe blinked again. "Vanity" was a word often heard in the Great Ga'Hoole Tree since the arrival of the strange blue owl, the Striga, from the newly discovered Middle Kingdom. But the owls of the great tree were deeply indebted to Striga, or "the Striga" as he preferred to be called, especially her parents, Soren and Pelli, and her sisters, Blythe and Bash. This blue-feathered owl had saved the life of little Bell. The Striga had flown across the Sea of Vastness and encountered Bell, who had been caught in a freak storm while out on a routine chawlet-training mission. She had been blown off course and injured. Had she not been found by the Striga she might have died. But that was only the beginning of Bell's trials. During her recovery, she and the Striga were captured by the Pure Ones and held hostage in the Desert of Kuneer. For many moon cycles there had been no news of the Pure Ones and their maniacal leader, Nyra. It was thought they had been vanquished, that only a remnant survived, and perhaps even that Nyra had been killed. But such was not the case. They had found new recruits, gone underground in the Kuneer Desert, and built themselves an elaborate system of underground nest holes and tunnels mastermined by Tarn, a wily Burrowing Owl.

The Striga and Bell managed to escape, but during the course of their captivity they had learned of a dreadful plan, a plan to assassinate the Band and the great tree's king, Coryn. This would have been a fatal blow to the very gizzard of the Great Ga'Hoole Tree. Had it not been for the Striga, all might have been lost. So it was not just Bell who owed her life to the strange blue owl, but the great tree itself. The Band and Coryn felt so indebted that they issued an invitation to the Striga: If he desired to come to the great tree he would be welcomed. Thus, after many moon cycles, the Striga had arrived, leaving the Middle Kingdom and the strange Dragon Court, where he had lived a pampered life of indescribable luxury and indolence.

"Look," Bell said excitedly, "you just give this singing up for the Harvest Festival and you'll get a blue feather from the Striga."

"Why would I want some old molted blue feather?" Blythe asked.

"It means you belong to the club, Blythe. The Blue Feather Club. Don't you want to be a member? Clubs are fun."

Blythe swiveled her head toward her younger sister. She didn't know what to say. Why were clubs so much fun? Singing was fun. *Bell just isn't the same anymore,* Blythe thought.

"I don't get it," Twilight said grumpily.

"Get what?" Gylfie asked.

The Great Gray Owl turned his head and peered into the tiny Elf Owl's eyes. "Now tell me truthfully, Gylfie. Does this seem like the night before the Harvest Festival to you? Where are the milkberry vine decorations?"

"And where's the milkberry brew?" Digger said, flying up to a perch in the main gallery in the Great Hollow. "I don't smell it brewing. And the harp guild hasn't been practicing at all. Seems like more of a Final ceremony than the merriest festival of the year."

"Agreed," said Soren. "Although I have to say that last year things *did* get a bit wild. I mean, did you ever in all your hatched days think you'd see Otulissa getting tipsy? She nearly squashed Martin."

"She loves to dance, though. I remember when she got you doing the glauc-glauc that first year we were all here," Digger said.

"I was not tipsy!" Otulissa swooped down from an upper gallery. "Ask Martin. He was the one who stumbled mid-flight. If anybody can hold their milkberry wine, it's me."

"Yeah, but I think someone really did spike it with some bingle juice and the two don't mix — at all!" Gylfie said. "It's a bad combination. Gives me indigestion. And those autumn mice, my favorite, repeating on me for the next three nights after I drank the stuff. Makes me burp to even think about it now."

"It's because of your size, Gylf," Twilight said. "You're just too small to handle bingle juice — in any form."

"Oh, now let's just cut out the small-stature remarks," Gylfie replied, sharply casting a harsh look at Twilight. As the tiniest of the Band she was sensitive about her size. In fact she had resurrected the SOS — the Small Owl

Society. It had been founded by Gylfie's grandmother, and its charter was to prevent cruel and tasteless remarks about size.

"Gylfie," Otulissa said, "this is not a reflection on your character. It is a scientific fact that smaller owls have a lower tolerance for milkberry wine and bingle juice. There is even a formula: You take your weight, multiply it by the square root of your wingspan, and then divide it by your head-to-tail length and that gives you the number of drams you can tolerate. Very simple. Your capacity is small. Maybe one one-tenth of a dram."

"I find this conversation infuriating," Gylfie fumed. "You're the one who stumbled in the glauc-glauc. Madame Plonk, who is nearly as big as Twilight, passes out every year. All I do is burp — and you've got me pegged as a tippler."

"I have said no such thing," Otulissa protested. "I was merely giving you the formula to calculate your capacity."

"Well," Digger said wearily, "no such formulas are going to be needed this year because it appears that no milkberry wine is being brewed."

"As a matter of fact," Otulissa said, "it appears to me that nothing is being done for the Harvest Festival. A big fat nothing!" Otulissa was rarely so unrefined in her pronouncements. The four owls all swiveled their heads toward Soren. He wilfed a bit.

"I know . . . I know. The Striga is a bit strange. I think we just have to be patient while Coryn figures out what to do with him." Soren resisted saying how indebted they all were to the blue owl. He did not need to constantly remind them of what he and Pelli owed to the Striga. They knew.

"But what does Coryn say?" Gylfie asked. "He seems sort of listless and distracted since our return from the Middle Kingdom. He should be rejoicing. We escaped the slink melf. The kingdom is intact. Not only that, we have a wonderful new ally in the Middle Kingdom. There is so much to be grateful for and yet he hardly ever comes out of his hollow these days."

"Got the gollymopes, I'd say," Digger offered. "Gone all broody on us — and I don't mean 'broody' as in sitting on an egg nest."

Gylfie blinked. Her yellow eyes grew bright. "You just gave me an idea, Digger!"

"Yeah, what's that?"

"Maybe we need to find Coryn a mate. He could use a little romance in his life."

"Not a bad idea," Twilight said thoughtfully. "He needs to settle down. Have some companionship in the hollow."

"Speak for yourself." Soren laughed. Of all the Band, Soren was the only one who had thus far found a mate.

"Oh, Soren, you know me. I play the sky! I'm not the settling-down type," Twilight said. The other owls flashed quick, knowing looks to one another. They knew exactly what was coming. "You know me. I'm a product of the Orphan School of Tough Learning. I'd be terrible at coddling hatchlings."

"I think," Soren said softly, "you'd be a lot better than you imagine."

"What in the name of Glaux are those owlets doing?" Otulissa suddenly asked as she caught a glimpse of a half dozen owlets flying around with feathery blue tufts in their talons.

"Oh, it's something called the Blue Feather Club," Soren said. "It's a fad. It will pass. Bell wants Blythe and Bash to join."

"Is Blythe going to sing at the Harvest Festival, Soren?" Gylfie asked.

"Yes, Madame Plonk says Blythe's a natural even though she's not a Snowy. I do hope she gets to sing. She's been practicing so hard. But . . ." There was a wistful note in Soren's voice.

"But what?" Gylfie asked.

"Oh, nothing, nothing really," Soren replied.

But Gylfie, who knew Soren best of all, sensed that there was something worrying Soren deeply.

CHAPTER TWO

Why a Blue Feather?

Blythe would not be allowed to sing. There would be no bingle juice, no dancing. One would hardly know it was a festival. Worst of all, this was by order of Coryn. "Just this once, that's all," Coryn had said. "You know how much we owe him. It seems the right thing to do." That was Coryn's reasoning for the pared-down Harvest Festival.

The Band exchanged glances as they perched in Coryn's hollow, and Coryn looked nervously from one to the other. "You understand, don't you?"

"Not really," Twilight replied bluntly.

"Don't be difficult, Twilight," Coryn said.

"I am not being difficult. I really don't understand."

"I don't understand where the Striga gets the right," Gylfie added.

Coryn drew himself up a bit taller and puffed out his chest feathers. "It has nothing to do with rights. Look, do any of us have to be reminded of how awful it was not much more than a year ago during the time of the Golden

Tree? The cult of the ember? The Guardians of this tree became obsessed with pomp and ceremony. They began to worship the Ember of Hoole. It was terrible. All that gilt and glitter had nothing to do with being an owl. It was Other-ish. You were the first to say it, Soren."

Soren blinked. Coryn was right. They should be suspect of ritual. The Striga had roused himself from the jeweled splendor, the listless existence at the Dragon Court. Condemning luxury and pampering, he had endured the extreme pain of stripping out his own excess of feathers. Yes, this owl was definitely wary of excess, of indulgence, of the vulgarities that came with celebrations and festivities. These thoughts ran through Soren's mind while Coryn spoke. Soren had to admit that it had been extremely astute of Coryn to refer to the time of the Golden Tree and the pernicious consequences of ritual and celebration that had inspired the cult of the ember.

The Band, as they often did, looked to Soren. It was from Soren that they usually took their cue in matters to do with Coryn, for the young king was Soren's nephew. "You have raised some interesting points, Coryn. For now, we will respect your wishes."

Twilight blinked, barely disguising the glare in his eyes. "Will there be a Punkie Night?"

"Of course," Coryn said. Punkie Night was celebrated

on the first new moon after the Milkberry Harvest Festival. It was a favorite holiday, especially for fledglings, although grown-up owls got into the spirit almost as much as the young'uns. There were mischief and sweets and masks. Bands of young owls put on masks and flew from the hollow, and, in exchange for sweets, they would sing or do flying acrobatic tricks. Although Twilight was much too old for such frolicking, it didn't stop him. He was one of the most enthusiastic and raucous punkies. Donning the mask of a Pygmy Owl, he flew about with the fledglings, egging them on with his antics.

"There better be a Punkie Night. What's life without a bit of punk?" Twilight muttered as he left Coryn's hollow with the rest of the Band.

Soren was the last to leave. And before he hopped out the port to the branch, he turned to his nephew and blinked several times. "You're sure about this, are you, Coryn?"

"Yes, Uncle. We must be wary of ritual and ceremony...." Soren was only half listening because something in Coryn's hollow had caught his attention, something that he had not noticed before. Wedged into one of the niches where Coryn kept some of his favorite things was the tip of a blue feather. *Why in the name of Glaux would Coryn keep a molted blue feather? That club is for young'uns. Coryn's not an owlet.*

CHAPTER THREE

An Odd Conversation

Otulissa had not gone to Coryn's hollow for the conference. In addition to her other duties, which were many, she had temporarily taken on the job of chief librarian when Winifred's, an ancient Barred Owl, arthritis had kicked up. So while the Band had been discussing the Harvest Festival with Coryn, Otulissa was minding the library. This was a job she loved, for it afforded her the opportunity to further her research on a weather-interpretation project she had been pursuing since her return from the Middle Kingdom — windkins and the system of air known as the River of Wind that flowed between the Ga'Hoolian world and the Middle Kingdom. Otulissa's powers of concentration were great. She did not hear the clutch of little owlets giggling over a joke book nor did she hear the owl approaching the desk where she perched. It was actually the desk of Ezylryb, the late distinguished ryb, scholar, poet, historian, and, once upon a time, great warrior of the tree.

"Ahem." The owl cleared his throat. Otulissa's head jerked up from her labors. The blue owl, the Striga, perched before her.

"Oh, so sorry. I was quite absorbed here," Otulissa said.

"I didn't mean to disturb you."

But you did, thought Otulissa. She had little tolerance for the indiscriminate use of words. *Wouldn't it have been better to say simply, "Sorry to disturb you"?*

"What is it, might I ask, that absorbs you so?" the Striga asked.

"I have for some time been immersed in a study of weather and air currents. I am a member of the weather-interpretation chaw."

"Oh," the Striga said with a jovial note in his voice. "I approve!"

Otulissa blinked. She did not quite understand. "Approve of what?" she cocked her head to one side. *What in the name of Glaux is there to approve of? And why should you be the one doing the approving?* But she, of course, said none of this aloud.

"I approve of the practical studies such as weather." He swung his head slowly around. "But not the inessential, the frivolous, the, how should I put it? The heretical texts."

"Heretical?"

"Yes. You know, the anti-Glaux books such as those the young owlets are giggling over." He nodded toward the young owls gathered around a desk reading a book with great glee.

"It's a joke book! That's all!" Otulissa then told one of the few lies she had ever told in her life. "I read it myself when I was an owlet." Otulissa had never read a joke book, but she would never deny another owl the right to read one.

"But such books are fripperies, indulgences, vanities!"

She looked at him closely. *What is this owl talking about?* This word "vanity" was often in his speech.

"I am not quite sure what you mean by the word 'vanity' in reference to literature."

"Literature?" He paused. "But surely, Otulissa, you need not concern yourself with literature, for you are a student of practical disciplines — like this er ... uh ... weather and — what is it you are reading now?"

She didn't like the way he asked the question. It was interfering, beaky. Why should she have to tell him what she was reading or studying? It wasn't as if she had anything to hide. In fact, she was quite proud of this book, because it had been written by one of her own ancestors, a most distinguished scholar, the most renowned weathertrix of the previous century, Strix Emerilla. The book had the rather ponderous title *Atmospheric Pressures and Turbulations: An Interpreter's Guide*. She held it up. "Written by my thrice-great-aunt, maternal side."

"You must be proud," the Striga answered softly.

"I am. I am very proud," Otulissa replied curtly.

"You must be careful of too much pride."

"Another vanity?" Otulissa leaned forward a bit and peered more closely at him. His face looked different from when he had first arrived at the tree. The feathers had thinned. Indeed, his face was almost bald. There was just a thin mist of blue over the gray-and-puckered skin.

"Exactly, Otulissa! Exactly!"

Otulissa flexed her head to one side, then to the other, running through a series of head postures as if she were studying the blue owl from every possible angle.

"I am curious," Otulissa began in a reflective tone. "Just what do you mean by this word 'vanity'?"

"Oh, I am so glad you asked."

I'm sure you are! Otulissa thought to herself.

"As you know, Otulissa, I came from the Dragon Court, a most impractical place." The Striga gave special emphasis to the word "impractical." "It had become this way because of excess — excess of luxuries, of pampering, of every kind of indulgence imaginable. At the very center of this excess, the driving force, the fuel that fired it, was vanity."

"But what is vanity?" Otulissa asked.

"Vanities are all the indecent things in life, the fripperies, the impracticalities that distract us from Glaux and our true owlness."

"True owlness?" Otulissa blinked.

"Yes, we are, by nature, humble creatures."

"Hmm." Otulissa sniffed, and thought of Twilight. *Humble, my talon!*

"We must practice humility," the Striga continued. "Anything else is vanity."

Otulissa was tempted to say, *Well, to each his own.* But she thought better of it. "One last question," she said.

"Of course."

Her eyes fastened on his face. "Are you suffering from mite blight? I notice the feathers on your face are quite thin."

"Oh, nothing of the sort," the Striga answered almost cheerfully. "No. You see, for a long time, I was burdened with an indecent abundance of feathers. These feathers were the ultimate vanity. We dragon owls cultivated them with a disgusting mixture of pride and pleasure, preening all day. There were even special servants whose only job was to stroke and comb our feathers." The Striga seemed to wilf just talking about it. "I can't tell you how vile it was."

"But you did it. You preened your long blue feathers," Otulissa said curtly.

"I knew nothing better. I was deluded," the Striga said.

Otulissa blinked. There was so much that she did not understand about the Panqua Palace and the Dragon Court. She thought of Theo, that noble owl from ancient times they had all read about in the legends. When Otulissa had been in the Middle Kingdom, she had learned that it was Theo who had realized that the best way to distract owls with evil intentions, was to engulf them in luxury. The result was overweening vanity, so that their attention could focus only on one thing — themselves — to the point where they were reduced to powerlessness. It was an ingenious strategy for quelling the most dangerous kinds of owls, which had found their way into the Middle Kingdom long ago.

"But I still don't understand," Otulissa said to the Striga. "You now have fewer feathers than any of us. Especially on your face."

"I strip them out. It is my personal penance. Thus I relinquish the unnecessary things, the distractions."

"I've never thought of feathers as a distraction, frankly. They are a most essential part of our bodies." She paused. "Our true owlness, as it were." She emphasized the word "owlness."

"But not your spirit! And how can the spirit rise, become everlasting, when burdened by the vanities of feather and bone?" The Striga blinked his pale yellow eyes.

What did the Striga mean by "everlasting"? Life was the here and now. One must be able to rise into the air above this earth and fly. Was it not an abuse to pluck the very gifts Glaux had given owls to make a life for themselves? But Otulissa, for whom arguments were like a tonic, had no desire to engage in any further discussion with the Striga on the subject. Indeed, after this odd conversation, Otulissa was rendered speechless for one of the very few times in her life.

CHAPTER FOUR

Simplicity

Otulissa was not the only one that early evening who had entered into a very odd conversation. When the Band left Coryn's hollow, the young king felt as if something rather strange had occurred. It was almost as if it was not he himself speaking. But it was. He, of all of them, had spent the most time with the Striga since he had arrived at the great tree. Although their lives had been entirely different and Coryn had never lived in anything comparable to the Dragon Court of the Panqua Palace, he somehow sensed a resonance with what this owl had been saying. Coryn's early life in the harsh, unforgiving landscape of canyonlands had been entirely different from the Dragon Court. He had never been pampered, and had been abused by his mother, who had subjected him to a merciless indoctrination in order to make him a leader of the Pure Ones. The two words, "Pure Ones," almost carried a stench. For the Pure Ones believed that Barn Owls, *Tyto albas*, were the only true owls. The rest were impure, inferior, afflictions to owlkind. It was a base, venal notion. The violence that could be justified by such thinking was revealed to Coryn most brutally when, before his eyes, his mother killed his only friend.

But then the Striga had come to the great tree, invited by Soren and the rest of the Band after the defeat of Nyra and the Pure Ones in the Middle Kingdom. He had fought bravely, if not strictly according to the fighting methods practiced by the owls of the Middle Kingdom. The Striga's attack had been bloody and the Hoolian owls were in his debt.

The Striga preached that within every owl there was a "perfect simplicity." But to find it, one must cleanse — or "scour" — one's self of vanities and fripperies and all such distractions, and then a level of perfect simplicity would be attained. And thus, the message was an uncomplicated one: Burn away vanity. Being truly cleansed, one would achieve the supreme state of perfect simplicity, ready to receive Glaux's blessings forever and ever.

Just as Coryn was thinking about this, the Striga entered.

"How did it go?" the Striga asked.

"I'm not really sure."

"They agreed?"

"Yes," Coryn replied.

"Well, that's good."

"Yes, it is." Coryn nodded his head vigorously, almost as if he was trying to convince himself. "It is. Yes, I'm sure it is. But . . ."

"But, what?" the Striga asked.

"Well, it's a change — this new way of celebrating the Harvest Festival. I promised them that we were just trying this. That we'd still have Punkie Night."

"Of course," the Striga said quickly, although he had no idea what Punkie Night was. He felt that now was not the time to push.

"I think Soren felt a little bad about Blythe not singing."

"She will sing better when she has achieved simplicity. Then it will not be a vain art." The Striga paused. "I was having a most interesting conversation in the library with Otulissa."

"Really?" Coryn looked up.

"She is a very intelligent owl."

"She's practically a genius!" Coryn said.

"Yes, well, you know she has embarked on a very — very interesting research project."

"Oh, yes. Her study of windkins and the currents in the River of Wind. She and Soren are veterans of the weather-interpretation chaw, and were taught by the old master Ezylryb himself."

"I think these studies are good. Practical. Would it not be a benefit to the tree if she were allowed to pursue them further?"

"Well, yes. She had talked about going out and performing some experiments, some feather-drift trials."

"Feather drift?" Striga asked.

"Yes. It is done with wind and air currents. Feather buoys are set out, then tracked to measure variations in speed and drift."

"And who does it? Just the weather chaw?"

"Well, it's mostly under Otulissa's direction but, you know, it's fun. So, oftentimes, the rest of the Band goes. I mean, that is one thing that is special about the Band. They are so talented that they can really serve in any chaw when called upon. Gylfie, she's chief ryb of the navigation chaw, so she can take instant fixes on the positions as the feathers drift. Digger is a skilled tracker, as is Twilight. Both come in handy."

"Might I propose something, Coryn?"

"Certainly."

"Do you think it might take their minds off this simplified Harvest Festival if they were on a mission?"

Coryn's eyes suddenly brightened. "You mean, perhaps Otulissa and the Band should go on a research expedition for her study of windkins?"

"Precisely. A service that they will rise to joyfully and it might . . . oh, how should I say, distract them from their regrets about the Harvest Festival."

"It's a wonderful idea. I'll send for them right now," Coryn said.

The Striga raised a talon in the air as if to caution him. "And when you tell them about this experiment, try to convey to them how essential this is to the well-being of the tree. How they are really the only owls who could do this because of their extraordinary expertise, brilliance, and depth of knowledge. Impress upon them that they are the best and that these studies are crucial. As a matter of fact, why not make the announcement in the parliament to give it the dignity it deserves?"

"You're absolutely right. The parliament! That is where it should be announced."

Coryn regarded the Striga with even deeper respect. It was a splendid idea, but more moving to Coryn was that the Striga valued Otulissa's research. That truly surprised him. He wished that the Band could have heard the Striga's concern for their feelings. *I think they judge him too harshly,* Coryn thought. *Had they only been here! But give them time, give them time. They will see, as I have, that this is an owl of many parts. Good parts, all of them!*

CHAPTER FIVE

Windkins, Advanced Study of

I've called this meeting of the parliament tonight to put forth a proposal," Coryn began.

"If this has anything to do with scrapping Punkie Night, I'm out of here!" Twilight muttered.

"Hush!" Soren said, and shot the Great Gray a severe look.

"As we know, Otulissa is our greatest scholar."

The Striga noticed that the Spotted Owl swelled a bit. *Good!*

"Her intellect," Coryn continued, "is renowned throughout the kingdoms of owls, including the Middle Kingdom. But the Band, as well, are fine students of our natural world, and that is why I have brought you together to approve this plan."

Something about all this just did not sound right to Soren. He couldn't put his talon on it, and so continued to listen. But why hadn't Coryn mentioned this plan to him or the Band before now? It certainly seemed to involve them.

"For some time," Coryn continued, "Otulissa has been studying the windkin patterns of the River of the Wind." Otulissa's face became more alert. "What I propose now is that the Band, with Otulissa as the expedition leader, set out now to gather information. . . ."

"Data," Otulissa interjected. *And why didn't Coryn consult me before announcing it?* she wondered.

"Data," Coryn continued, "that might further these studies. We must understand that these are the best, the brightest, the most insightful owls . . ."

Stop with the adjectives already, Soren thought. *Flattery. Why is he trying to flatter us like this?* But the proposal was tempting nonetheless. Some of his fondest memories were of the weather expeditions on which Ezylryb had sent them.

Otulissa raised her talon and stepped from her parliamentary position on the curved white branch where the members perched in a half circle. "May I say something? I am of course fl —" She a felt an alarming jerk in her gizzard and paused, mid-speech. "Flattered," she continued softly. A bilious sensation rose in her gorge as she said the word. ". . . first of all, that you find my work interesting and important. As much as I would love to lead this expedition, I do not think at this time it is possible."

The Striga blinked. He had not expected this.

"My duties here at the tree," Otulissa went on, "especially since Winifred has been perched up with her arthritis, are great." The Striga tried not to wilf. "My real job is to interpret the data, work it into my theoretical framework, and then derive applicable ..." Otulissa was off and flying on how responsible science was performed. The upshot was that the Band would go, but Otulissa would not.

"So," Otulissa said when the Band had reconvened in the library. "A brief explanation here about my work." She hauled out the Strix Emerilla book and several other scientific books, along with a variety of charts and some old scrolls written by Ezylryb when he had lived in the Northern Kingdoms and wrote as Lyze of Kiel.

"*History of the Ice Claw Wars?*" Digger said. "Why? And the *Sonnets of the Northern Kingdoms?*"

"Would you believe that the first time I ever heard of the word 'windkin' was in a sonnet Lyze had written to his mate, Lil? He spoke of them like a pair of windkins, interlocking, harmonious despite any distance. You see, as a scientist and a scholar, I cannot afford to discard anything. I must read everything — science, poetry, history — if it will help." She paused and said suddenly, "Even joke books!"

"Joke books?" They all chuckled.

"Whatever do you mean?" Gylfie asked.

Otulissa looked down at her talons and shook her shoulders. "I'm not really sure what I meant by that. But you get the point. One has to read and think outside the usual, predictable ways."

"And just what are your hunches about these windkins?" Soren asked.

"And where is it you want us to explore?" Gylfie asked.

"I want you to try to pinpoint their locations and do some drift analysis. My coordinates show that there is a possibility of windlets in the Shadow Forest. So, I would like you to go there. You'll need the usual tools — feather buoys, air floaters, tethers, and, of course, the thermoscope." The thermoscope was a clever device that Ezylryb had invented for measuring changes in temperature. She paused and then looked out the hollow of the library. A nearly full moon was rising. "Well," she sighed, "I suppose you should be on your way soon. Look at that moon! It's so beautiful. But I don't think you'll be missing much of a Harvest Festival here."

"And we shall certainly be back in time for Punkie Night." Twilight thumped his talon for emphasis.

Otulissa saw them off from the main branch of the library, watching the four owls lift into flight, their silhouettes printed against the rising moon. Normally, she would have been bubbling with excitement that she was sending off someone to carry out her experiments. But tonight, she did not feel that familiar fever of anticipation. She decided she needed to get out of the library for a while and go to her favorite place for reflection, her hanging garden. If she had not started the garden, another owl would have. High in the great tree, leaves and other bits of organic matter had collected in crevices called "trunk pockets," which, over the ages, had decayed into soil. And into these little patches of earth, seedlings had found their way. Huckleberry mostly. In the lower canopy of the tree, there was a tree-pocket garden that Otulissa thought of as her own, and she tended it lovingly.

Otulissa discovered that many plants that grew on the ground could grow in the trunk pockets of the great tree. She had brought flowering plants, moss, lichens, even orchids to her hanging garden. Settling down amid the hanging lichens, beneath a clump of lovely liverwort that was spinning in shards of moonlight, she wondered about her lack of excitement over the Band's expedition. That delicious fizzy feeling she often experienced on the path of discovery was simply not there. If anything, she felt flat and apprehensive. She had stayed behind not just because of her duties. Winifred's arthritis was a convenient excuse. No, it was something else. Why had she mentioned joke books when she had delivered her little speech about how one must read widely? It wasn't just the diminished Harvest Festival that troubled her. For some reason, a large part of her anxiety seemed to be related to the library. The library and her precious books. *No*, she corrected herself, *they are not just* my *books. They are everyone's.*

Just then, one of the matrons appeared, a bunchy Barred Owl named Glynnis. The matron owls often tended the younger owlets, and worked in the infirmary and the kitchen of the great tree. "Want a spot of milkberry tea, Otulissa?" she offered. "I have a little left in this pot, and you've got a cup there, haven't you? Chill in the air."

"Oh, that would be lovely, Glynnis," Otulissa said.

"Working late?" Glynnis said as she poured the tea.

"Yes, yes. I just have some things to attend to in the library." Otulissa took a sip of tea and felt a twinge, possibly of defiance, she thought, well up in her gizzard. So much for the calming effects of the hanging garden. She set down her cup, thanked Glynnis, and flew down to the library. She made her way to the back shelves where the young owlets had been perching earlier. She had intended to pluck down the joke book they had been reading, and then she spotted another called *Slightly Filthy Riddles for Soiled Minds.* She had never read any such fare in her life. But she, after all, was an advocate of reading widely. She only wished that the owl who called himself "the Striga" would appear right this minute and see her. There was one entire chapter devoted to wet poop jokes. She read the first one and began to chuckle.

> *There once was a seagull named Luke*
> *Who was hungry and craved some hot soup.*
> *He spied a swell fish, and exclaimed, "What a dish!"*
> *But spoiled it with a big splatty poop.*

Otulissa sighed. Such was the humor of very young owls, just the kind of jokes they loved to read and retell in the dining hollow, causing them to be dismissed immediately. *But perhaps*, Otulissa mused, *this kind of foolishness is good for us older owls, too, once in a while. What is that blue owl so wrought up about? Why are his so very few feathers in such a twist?*

CHAPTER SIX

Burnt Paper

The Band was on the wing again. They had made excellent time, and there was yet another hour left in the night until dawn. It felt good. *Almost too good*, thought Soren. It was somehow a relief to get away from the great tree. Pelli, his dear mate, seemed to understand implicitly, and even though he had told her that this was a scientific expedition, she sensed that there were other reasons he needed to be off for a while. She knew he was concerned about Coryn. Soren worried about the young king as much as he did about his own owlets. He was, after all, Coryn's uncle. Perhaps it was because Soren himself had been taken under wing by the revered Ezylryb that he felt he must do the same for Coryn. In Ezylryb, Soren had the finest role model one could have imagined. He attributed all the good things he had learned, all the qualities and virtues that made him the owl he now was, to the grizzled old ryb. And there was not a night that passed that he did not miss that old Whiskered Screech. If he could do as well by Coryn as Ezylryb had done for him, then all his worry would be worth it.

Coryn was an owl endowed with mysterious and great gifts. Throughout his entire youth, he had exhibited unparalleled courage against the worst odds imaginable, and had retrieved the Ember of Hoole from the volcanoes in the Beyond. Coryn's parents, Nyra and Kludd, were the vile, sadistic, crazed leaders of the Pure Ones. It was a terrible, daunting legacy to bear. One that Coryn, in his mind and heart and gizzard, battled with constantly. Secretly, Soren believed that Coryn had never sought a mate because he was terrified of passing on this bad blood.

And now Soren was again worried about his nephew. There had been bad times before, especially the dreadful time of the Golden Tree. Even though the ember was now safely hidden in Bubo's forge, ever since the Striga had arrived Coryn had been behaving strangely. Soren knew that Coryn was haunted by his mother, Nyra. It was unfortunate that her body had not been found in that last battle in the Middle Kingdom, but Soren felt that even if her death had been confirmed, it would not have made a difference in the way that Coryn was feeling.

Soren scanned the deep blue sky around him and pushed troubling thoughts from his mind. This whole business about the Harvest Festival was baffling. Perhaps he should have stood up to his nephew more firmly. Ah, well, too late for that. And this was an interesting expedition.

"Do you smell that?" Gylfie said as they approached the border between the Shadow Forest and Silverveil. It took them a minute, but then the others also picked up the odor of something burning.

"Not a forest fire," Soren noted. "Not the season for them."

"It doesn't smell like trees," Gylfie said.

Soren, who had the best hearing of any of the owls, angled his head as he tried to pick up any sound clues. "No sap popping." Evergreen trees and maples, which were becoming thicker in this region, were full of sap. As the sap in a burning tree heated up, a popping sound could be detected. In certain seasons when the sap was running, a burning tree could actually explode.

"Do you hear anything?" Digger asked.

"Not really. There were fires I think, but mostly small ones. And those are just smoldering now. It's hard to describe." The sounds of a dying fire were difficult to explain. To Soren, it sounded like a sighing, a slow stirring of ashes, almost expired embers losing their heat, the glow seeping from them. Of course, all it took for the fire to be roused and erupt into new life was a small maverick wind. But these fires, he felt, had been carefully wetted down. *Peculiar. Very peculiar*, he thought.

"Funny smell, isn't it?" Gylfie said.

"Yeah, I know what you mean," Digger said. "It's not like smoke from fires in the wild."

"Smells like paper," Soren said suddenly, then added, "burnt paper."

"Exactly!" said Gylfie.

Dawn was breaking by the time the Band settled into a hollow in a blue spruce. They were familiar with the tree from past visits to this forest. Twilight and Digger went out and hunted down a few ground squirrels because they were all hungry. The ground squirrels of the Shadow Forest were particularly tasty and known for their rich nutty flavor.

"Mmmm," said Twilight as he bit off the head of one.

"Yep, they're good," Gylfie said. But no one seemed particularly jovial despite the good food. In fact, there was little talk. They were tired. Just a few words and comments exchanged before they nestled down. This was not due to simple physical exhaustion. The flight had been an easy one. An anxiety seemed to hang in the air, an unspoken concern about what they had left behind at the great tree. It was almost midday before any of them fell asleep.

CHAPTER SEVEN
The Blue Feather Club

T his is so boring," Blythe muttered to her sister Bash. The three B's and several other young owls were in the foul-weather hollow — a play hollow for young owls when the weather was too bad for them to play outside. But tonight, the first night of the Harvest Festival, the weather was beautiful, the moon full, the breezes light. A perfect night for flying. The Striga had been calling off their names for attendance.

"Hush," Bell scolded. Blythe glared at her. Her sister had changed so much since the Striga had come to the tree.

It's the Harvest Festival, and I was supposed to be singing. Now I am standing here with this dumb blue feather! Blythe thought. Neither she nor Bash had ever heard the great tree so silent during a festival. Punkie Night was only a short moon cycle away. Would it be cancelled, too?

It better not be this way when Punkie Night comes along!

Blythe thought. She and Bash and all their friends had been practicing their four-point rolls. One had to master flying upside down and backward to really do them right. And Punkie Night was the perfect time to show off such tricks.

The three B's had only experienced one other Punkie Night in their lives and it was the year before, after they had first fledged. Now it was their favorite holiday and they loved flying around with their uncle Twilight, who went completely yoicks playing pranks on Punkie Night.

"I am very pleased to see you here," said the Striga, putting aside the roll call. He spoke to them from the main perch in the hollow. It all seemed so wrong. Normally on this first eve of the Harvest Festival, the music from the grass harp would be streaming out from the Great Hollow higher up in the tree as the nest-maid snakes of the harp guild wove themselves through its strings. Owls, young and old, would be fly-dancing through the milkberry vines that had turned the copper-rose color that gave this time of year its name, the season of the Copper-Rose. But an eerie stillness hung over the tree. *And I would be singing for the first time,* Blythe thought glumly.

"Can we see some smiles?" the Striga asked, looking directly at Blythe.

"Why?" Blythe replied sullenly.

"Well, that is what I'm going to explain, dear. I think you will have something to be cheerful about after I describe the perils of the world I came from and the new joys I have found on my journey toward simplicity as I have cast off my vanities."

"There's a little bit of blood above your eye," said Justin, a tiny Northern Saw-whet. Justin was just a hatchling, the first nestling of Martin and his mate, Gemma.

"That's part of my story," replied the Striga. "You see, once upon a time, I was an owl in the Dragon Court. We did nothing all day long except preen. In fact, we did not even do most of the preening ourselves but had special servants to do it." Several owlets giggled at this. But not Blythe. Nor Bash.

"That's silly," said a new hatchling, who still looked like a fuzz-ball with her owlet's down.

"But what about the blood?" Blythe persisted.

"Don't interrupt, Blythe," Bell hissed. "You're embarrassing me!"

"I'm getting to that, dear."

Blythe felt an uncomfortable twinge in her gizzard. This Striga had no right to call her "dear." Only her mum and da could call her "dear" — and Mrs. P.! "You see, because of this excessive preening, the deep luxury, the vanities . . ." The Striga sighed as if the very thought gave him indescribable pain.

I knew that word "vanities" was coming, Blythe thought, and exchanged glances with Bash. They had gone to the library and looked up the word in the *Strix Standard Hoolian Dictionary,* and not the owlet version, either, the baby one for beginning readers.

The Striga continued talking. "Because of that my feathers came in thickly and grew to extraordinary lengths."

"Didn't you ever molt?" Justin asked.

"Rarely, and only lightly. That is one of the best parts of my life here. Now I molt like a normal owl."

There is nothing "normal" about this owl, Blythe thought.

"Even now, however, my molts continue to be light. So I just help them along by plucking out my feathers. Hence, this speck of blood."

"What does 'hence' mean?" a hatchling whispered.

"It means 'because,'" Bash whispered back.

"Doesn't it hurt?" asked Heggety, a Short-eared Owl. "The plucking?"

The Striga cocked his head slightly and churred softly. "Not really, my dear. It is, how should I put it? A rewarding sort of pain, a cleansing sort of agony. Not nearly as horrid as the vanity that grew these feathers."

This is just plain weird! Blythe thought. She wished that she and Bash hadn't come. But they had promised Bell that they would at least attend one meeting of the Blue Feather Club. And Bell had been so thrilled. She apparently got points for each new member she brought in. When Bash had asked what the points were for, Bell hemmed and hawed and really could not give her an answer. Both Bash and Blythe were simply confounded by the change in Bell. Why did she want points or anything else from this blue owl? Yes, he had saved her life, nursed her when she was wounded, but this all seemed a bit much. Nonetheless, they were here now and Blythe would try to make the best of it. But by Glaux, Blythe knew she wasn't going to join the club, and she'd be surprised if Bash did.

"And when we cast off the vanities," the Striga went on, "we become favored by Glaux and upon our deaths will ascend straight to glaumora."

"But that's a long time off," Justin said. "I've hardly started to budge my primaries."

"Oh, but that is where you're wrong, my dear. The night of the Great Scouring is coming, bringing death to all but a few."

"Only a few?" asked Heggety. "Who chooses the few? What happens to *them*? Who decides?"

"Oh, that's the good part, dear. The few who have renounced the vanities will be swept up directly to glau-mora." The Striga ignored Heggety's last question.

Blythe looked around. She saw that many of the little owlets and hatchlings were beginning to tear up. *This is not good*, she thought. *Is this why Bell is trying to make us join this club? Has this stupid owl scared Bell with all his talk of death? It doesn't amount to a pile of racdrops. I hate this owl!* If only she were bigger, she would pop the blue owl a good one, smack in his beak.

"Why? Why?" Blythe asked in a loud voice. "Why would this Great Scouring be happening? Why should we all die young or get swept up?"

The Striga looked sternly at her. "The great tree has been suffering. You have heard your parents speak of the time of the Golden Tree, of ornamentation and excess and, indeed, shame. I think that Glaux has chosen this tree and its noble Guardians to lead the way. And you children must lead the grown-ups by taking this pledge to swear off these vanities, and each of you will get your blue feather and become a member of the club. Come, come!" He motioned with his threadbare wing.

"I don't know how he flies with that thing!" Blythe whispered. But he did. For one who could barely get off the ground when he was in the Dragon Court he had become a strong flier. She blinked when she saw how many little owls were hopping toward where the Striga perched with his bundle of feathers. But she and her sister Bash clutched firmly to their perches and did not move.

"Now, repeat after me: 'I do solemnly swear on my gizzard and all that I hold most dear, to give up the vanities, false treasures, and fripperies so I might attain perfect simplicity and escape the Great Scouring. . . .'"

Blythe and Bash looked in astonishment as they saw owlets give up their precious acorn necklaces, their fragments of stained glass from old chapels of the Others, special pebbles they had found. Some of the older owlets who had earned merit badges in chawlet practices gave even them up. *Forget about it! If this frinkin' owl thinks I'm giving up my merit badge from flying that mini squall in weather interpretation, he's got another thing coming!* thought Blythe.

"What is going on here? A Final ceremony?" Trader Mags gasped as she swooped in on the tree and alighted on the branch just outside of Ezylryb's hollow, where Octavia, the rather fat, elderly nest-maid snake still lived. The magpie could not have chosen a worse time to appear, for it was precisely the moment when the young owlets were giving up their "vanities" in the foul-weather hollow and instead of music flowing from the tree on this night of the Harvest Festival, there was utter silence. Octavia poked her head out of the hollow. She waggled her head back and forth as if trying to find the right words to explain the situation to Mags. "Oh my! Oh my!" she sighed. "It's . . . uh . . . difficult to explain but I hope — we all hope — it's a passing thing." Octavia also served Madame Plonk and had been a member of the grass harp guild for many years.

"I don't get it," Trader Mags said.

Her assistant, the rather dim-witted Bubbles, appeared with the bundles. "Where are we to put these out, madam?"

"I don't think there will be much of a call for your goods tonight." Octavia sighed again.

Trader Mags was known throughout the Hoolian kingdoms as the foremost dealer in quality merchandise scavenged from the very best ruins of the Others. Her beady eyes now contracted until they were just pinpricks, and her gaze drilled into Octavia. Octavia was blind but had highly developed sensibilities. She could feel Trader Mags' piercing look.

"Does this have something to do with that blue owl?"

"Yes! You know about him?" Octavia replied, suddenly very alert. "He only got here maybe a moon cycle ago."

"He may have only gotten to the great tree a moon cycle ago, but he's been around my neck of the woods longer than that, believe me."

41

Octavia coiled up in alarm. "You better talk to Otulissa immediately!" she whispered.

Bubbles, no mental giant, squawked, "But we ain't never sold nothin' to Otulissa. She don't like geegaws."

"Well, tonight you might have something of interest to her," Octavia replied.

Trader Mags cuffed Bubbles. "She's not telling us to go to Otulissa to sell her anything, nincompoop." She adjusted her red bandanna. "Where is she?"

"In the library, I think, and if not there, try the hanging garden." Octavia slithered onto the branch from which she had been suspended and swirled her head around to detect vibrations of anyone who might be listening in. "Tell her that the Striga has been here longer than we thought, much longer," she whispered.

"And where is Bubo?" Trader Mags asked.

"In his cave, well into his cups, I imagine."

"You mean drunk?"

"Precisely." Octavia nodded.

"And what about the harp guild snakes? What are they doing tonight?"

"Not much!"

"This is unbelievable!" Trader Mags muttered.

"I wish," Octavia replied mournfully.

CHAPTER EIGHT

Deep Gizzardly Twinges

Trader Mags had quietly flown into the library and taken up a perch as Fritha was proofreading *The Evening Hoot*. "Oh, Mags, I didn't hear you come in," Otulissa said. "I'm afraid you won't be doing much business here tonight." Although Otulissa had always been one of the magpie's most severe critics, she had gained a new respect for her in recent times. Mags had been most helpful just after Coryn had retrieved the ember and become king. It was a time sometimes referred to as the Great Flourishing. Mags had been invaluable in procuring many articles that were needed at the tree for new devices and tools they were building, which ranged from scientific instruments to parts for a printing press. The owls of the tree were now able to reproduce books and other literary matter. There would have been no *Evening Hoot* had the press not been assembled.

"So I gather. But Octavia thought I should come speak to you."

"About what?" Otulissa asked.

"This blue owl fella. Octavia thought you'd like to know he's been around longer than you think."

"What do you mean by that?" Otulissa was suddenly alert.

"Well, he might have just got to the great tree when the moon was newing. But he'd been on the mainland for a whole moon cycle before that."

"He was?" Otulissa blinked. "Where?"

"Here, there, everywhere." The magpie tossed her head about as she said the words. "You know, I get around. I get as much information as any slipgizzle in my line of work."

"So, what do you hear?" Otulissa asked thoughtfully.

"Younger ones are quite caught up with him. You know, the blue feathers and all."

Otulissa felt something clench in her gizzard. "A Blue Feather Club?" she asked in a somewhat tremulous voice.

"Yes, they call it something like that. Or maybe it's called the Blue Brigade."

"He's started something here, too," Fritha said.

"Do you know what they do?" Otulissa asked Mags. "This Blue Whatever?"

"Not much. They always have a small ground fire, though, at their meetings."

"A small ground fire?" Fritha and Otulissa both said at once. Ground fires made on purpose in the wild by owls were very odd. In the great tree, fires were for cooking, illumination, and, of course, Bubo had his powerful forge fires. "What would be the reason for these ground fires?" Otulissa asked.

"I'm not sure. Got to admit, I ain't got close enough to really see."

"Maybe they're just roasting squirrels or voles, out-door cooking," Fritha offered.

"Nobody cooks in the wild. We're the only ones who cook our meat," Otulissa said.

"No, it ain't roasted meat. That's not the smell. Sometimes it's a strange smell. I can't place it."

"Well, they certainly haven't been having ground fires around here," Otulissa huffed. "We would have noticed." But this did not set her mind at ease. She knew that since the blue owl had been at the great tree he had made flights to the mainland. Coryn explained that these were periods when the Striga felt a compelling need to be alone in the wilderness because he was overwhelmed by the worldliness of the tree. She supposed it might fit that the Striga felt too "full up" with the ways of the tree. But still, it was all very disturbing.

"And where do they get the fuel for these little ground

fires?" Otulissa suddenly asked. "Certainly these young owls belonging to the Blue Feather Clubs aren't seasoned colliers or blacksmiths."

"Oh, Otulissa, you show me a Rogue smith or a collier who doesn't want to make a bit on the side. And there is a buyer for everything. Take it from old Mags." Then the trader blinked suddenly with alarm.

"What is it?"

"I just remembered something." She shook her head in wonder. "I was flying over one of them dying ground fires, and something caught my eye. Thought it reminded me of something. Something sparkly but now all burnt up. I didn't pay it much heed at the time 'cause I was in a hurry."

"But what was it about the sparkly thing?" Otulissa asked.

"Well, ain't it simple enough? Most sparkly things, them glittery things that you don't like and Madame Plonk loves. Where else would they come from but me? And why would someone be trying to burn them up in a fire? Imagine them burning up perfectly wonderful treasures that I search all over creation for. Owls love my goods — why would they allow them to be burned?"

"I'm not sure," Otulissa said slowly, but once more she felt a twinge in her gizzard. "But I don't think those gems and jewels that sparkle would necessarily smell if they were burned."

"'Course not. But it weren't no burnt-cloth smell, either. Or any metal smell like you get when you're around a forge."

"What did it smell like? Can you think, Mags?"

"Maybe paper," the magpie replied.

At that moment, Fritha came up, looking a bit agitated. "Otulissa, I can't find that book of Lyze's poetry. No one's checked it out. I just wanted to quote something from it for the newspaper."

"And you know what else is missing?" Winifred, the ailing librarian, had just come in, flying rather lopsided due to her arthritic wing. "Couldn't find it for the life of me the other day."

"What's that?" Otulissa asked. She could feel her gizzard throbbing.

"Madame Plonk's book, *My Fabulous Life and Times: An Anecdotal History of a Life Devoted to Love and Song.* Cheers me up. You know I've been feeling so poorly. And I noticed a few of the other songbooks in that section were missing, too."

"Really?" Otulissa felt the throbbing stop and instead a terrible dread began to grow in her gizzard. "Excuse me," she said suddenly. "I have to go see Octavia immediately."

CHAPTER NINE

Visions of Hagsmire

Coryn had settled down in his hollow. It did feel odd not to be out celebrating on this night of full shine, the start of the Harvest Festival, but in another way there was a lovely peacefulness. He was perched studying the map of the Hoolian Kingdoms and the air currents above the Sea of Vastness. The Striga was perched solemnly across from him, studying the young king with his pale yellow eyes as Coryn studied the map and charts.

"Tell me, Coryn," the blue owl asked, "do you believe that glaumora is real?"

"Of course I do."

"And hagsmire?"

That was a hard question. Coryn was not really sure. Certainly, if there was one, he knew Kludd, his father, was there and would be condemned to it forever and ever. And if his mother, Nyra, was dead she would be there as well. But he preferred not to think of either of his parents in any kind of afterlife, glaumora or hagsmire. He just wanted them gone, their souls to evaporate into a complete and irrevocable nothingness. "I don't know," Coryn finally replied.

"But glaumora?" the Striga pressed.

"Oh, yes, yes. There must be a place for the good souls to go, the scrooms of decent owls."

"Decent owls?" the Striga said. "And what makes a decent owl?"

"Well, Hoole, the first king of this tree, was a great and decent owl. But one does not have to be great to be decent. One does not even have to be an owl."

Striga blinked in surprise at this. "What do you mean?"

"Well, for example, Mrs. Plithiver."

"The nest-maid snake?" the Striga replied, an edge of disgust in his voice.

"Yes."

"But she's a servant. She makes our life easier, more luxurious."

"Oh, but she's much more than that. She is a gifted musician and holds the highest rank in the harp guild as a sliptween."

"Yes," the Striga said coldly, and decided not to say more.

"And aside from that, she is a very good creature. She is sensitive and loving and wise. All those things."

A vain slithering thing, the Striga thought, *her music as useless as the baubles the awful tree singer, Madame Plonk, collects.* But he said none of this. Instead, he affected a very mournful gaze and looked down at his talons.

"You seem distressed, Striga," Coryn said anxiously.

"Does that matter to you?" the blue owl answered.

"Of course it matters. We owe you so much."

"You owe me nothing, but I owe it to you to share what I have learned; to share my vision of a world that might end — will end — on the night of the Great Scouring. I have seen it, Coryn."

Coryn suddenly wilfed, growing as slender as the branch he perched on.

"Let me tell you this, Coryn — you are your own worst enemy."

"How do you mean?" Coryn felt a sickening swirl in his gizzard. He thought he might yarp a very squishy half-digested pellet.

"Don't you see?" the Striga said.

"See what?"

"Hagsmire is real. You and I have both lived it. We both endured, survived, two very different kinds of hagsmire. I, in the Dragon Court, and you in the canyonlands as the hatchling of Nyra. You remember those times."

"How can I ever forget them?" Coryn had tried as a

young innocent owl to be everything that his mother had ever wanted. But he had not realized her lies, the true depth of her sadism, or how far she would go. She had tried to force him to murder his best friend, Phillip, and then killed the young Sooty Owl herself.

The Striga flew to the branch in the hollow where Coryn perched, so that his face was just inches away. He looked deep into Coryn's shining black eyes and saw his own reflection. "Don't you see? You and I share something. We have a bond, a bond like no other two owls." His voice had become rough with a new intensity. "In my hagsmire, I had a vision, a vision of a hagsmire to come. But there can be a glaumora for us if we are ready. I was chosen to survive in order to show the world this vision. And so were you. Who else has lived through hagsmire? Look at me, Coryn, my feathers once would have nearly filled this hollow and trailed out the port. And now I stand before you nearly scoured. And yet I fly, fly without ornamentation, without the vain trappings and fripperies in which I once luxuriated. And feathers were just the beginning of my vanities."

A small light like the flame of a candle flickered in Coryn's shining dark eyes. "We *have* shared something, haven't we?" Coryn spoke with a deep intensity and the Striga nodded. The young king thought about his hagsmire — a harsh country, cut with rock canyons. There was not a tree, not a meadow, but that harshness was nothing compared to the cruelty of his mother and her insane ambitions to raise him to be as ruthless and cruel as she was. And then there was the Striga's hagsmire — the resplendent palace where owls were so laden with feathers that they could hardly fly. Those foolish owls had become numb, without ambition for anything but their own pleasures. They had even mistaken that palace for glaumora, some said. All, that is, except for one owl, the Striga. Now that Coryn thought about it, the Striga's achievements were staggering. Coryn had fled harshness and cruelty in a barren landscape, but the Striga had abandoned luxury beyond measure, beyond imagination. How had he done it? This was an owl to be listened to. His talk of vanities was not idle.

"Tell me, Coryn." The Striga's voice had lost the intensity, the tautness, and agitation with which he had spoken moments before. His voice grew soft and had a lazy, almost casual tone. "Tell me about the ember."

CHAPTER TEN

Skart!

T here's one, down there!" Twilight called out.

"Finally!" Gylfie said. "Should I go for it, Digger?"

"Let's just see where it came from first."

For almost ten nights the Band had been in the southeastern part of the Shadow Forest pursuing their experiments for Otulissa. They had set out feather buoys to track the sources of the elusive feeder currents that Otulissa hypothesized were related to the River of Wind. So far, they had found none. Gylfie and Twilight flew into a low ground hover and focused on the tufts of feathery down that were slowly circulating inches above the ground. There was a green tag attached to one.

"Well," said Gylfie. "This is the one we set out three nights ago at a latitude of forty-three degrees north and one hundred twenty degrees west." Gylfie, the ryb of the navigation chaw and probably the best navigator in the history of the tree, had, over the past few years, advanced the science of navigation. By relating distance to time she had figured out how to derive a much more precise geographical location. While studying some fragmentary documents in the Palace of Mists, she stumbled upon the description of a little mechanism — a chronometer — for measuring time and immediately set about trying to build one. It was another instance in that time of the Great Flourishing when Trader Mags had been very helpful. In Mags' treasure trove, the chapel ruins in Silverveil where she lived, she had several of the key parts for the chronometer, and dedicated herself to searching the more distant ruins of the Others for the rest. Bubo helped by forging some of the tiny parts. Finally, such a clock, a very small one, had been reassembled.

There had been so many wonderful advances since Coryn had brought the Ember of Hoole to the Great Ga'Hoole Tree. That was part of the mystery of the ember. Its peculiar power bestowed both blessings and curses. The ember was neither purely good nor purely evil.

Twilight and Gylfie landed just beneath the still-circulating buoy. Gylfie flipped open the tiny chronometer that she always carried and did a few quick calculations.

"All right, yes! I think we have some interesting data here," Gylfie proclaimed triumphantly. "Let's get Digger and Soren."

"Yes!" Twilight hooted and thrust a talon into the air. "We win the prize!"

They had agreed that whoever made the first important finding got to eat the stomach of the next ground squirrel they caught. The stomach was the tastiest part of this delicious rodent, the prize.

Meanwhile, Soren and Digger were flying in another region of the Shadow Forest known as the "notch."

"I don't see them," Twilight said.

"I don't, either," Gylfie replied. Then suddenly from a very tall cedar, Soren appeared.

"Quick, follow me!" he said, swooping in. "I've been listening for you." His expression was grim.

"Did you find a feather buoy, or what?" Twilight asked. "Because if you did, it's a tie and we'll have to split the stomach."

"Forget about feather buoys. Follow me." Soren began to carve a steep, banking turn. It was a cloudy night and the moon was still in the newing phase, as it rose in the blackness like a thin curve of silver light scratching at the night. Soren swiveled his head around and addressed Twilight and Gylfie. "We're going to fly really high, and then begin to plunge. A stealth plunge."

A stealth plunge? Gylfie and Twilight both thought. This was a maneuver usually reserved for battle, not scientific expeditions. Whatever it was that Soren was leading them to must be serious. Soren launched himself into a climbing spiral, then a few minutes later began the plunge.

The target, however, was not an owl or prey, but rather one of the giant trees that could be found in the notch. They landed in the bushiest part of the tree, where Digger was waiting. He raised his port wing and signaled that they should be quiet. Then, with Digger now leading, they crept out on one of the branches. He indicated with his head to look down. There was indeed a peculiar scent. Something was burning below, but the smoke hung low over the ground. Gylfie and Twilight could not see what it was that Soren and Digger appeared to be focusing on, but a light breeze stirred the air, and the smoke cleared, leaving a blue-tinged gloom.

Within that gloom, they could see a circle of owls standing around a small fire. The owls' faces were bathed in the glow of the fire and their shadows danced across the pools of light behind them. Most of them were quite young. Some, however, were older. *Old enough to know better*, Soren thought. Digger and he had been astounded when they came across this queer ceremony. At first they were simply curious, but soon they felt a sickening twist in their gizzards as they watched a Burrowing Owl step up to the fire with a book in his beak and drop it into the flames. "Watch this!" Soren whispered to Gylfie. Another owl stepped forward and dropped in another book.

So this was the source of the smell, Gylfie thought. It was the smell she had been the first to detect as they approached the border between Silverveil and the Shadow Forest. Then another owl flew low over the fire. It was a Pygmy. She was young and in her beak was a strand of bright beads. She looked as if she were weeping and she hesitated as she held the beads. Another owl came up beside her and gave her a reassuring pat. Soren cocked his head to hear the words. "This is for the best. Those beads are a vanity. Give them up to the flames, dear, and when you do, they will burn and vanish with the smoke. Instead, in that space, a perfect simplicity will come and you shall be ready for glaumora on the night of the Great Scouring."

She's just a kid, Twilight thought. *This is obscene, skart!*

They saw the Pygmy finally drop the beads. Another owl presented her with a blue feather, and one to each of the four other owls, including the one who had dropped the book into the flames. The Band looked at one another in horror and felt a chill run through their gizzards. A cold wind seemed to blow through their hollow bones.

CHAPTER ELEVEN

Page by Page, Book by Book

On this same night, another pair of owls were wing-ing across the Sea of Hoolemere. Desperation filled them, their gizzards quivered in disgust. Their progress was slow, as the load that Otulissa and Fritha carried was a heavy one. Suspended beneath them in their talons were botkins of scrolls and strapped to their backs were books, smaller books in Fritha's case for she was a Pygmy Owl and too small to carry anything large on her back. Adding to their burden was an unfavorable wind. They would be lucky if they could make Cape Glaux by day-break. Otulissa would have welcomed more help but it would have only aroused suspicion. She had planned this operation meticulously, ever since that dreadful night when they had discovered the missing books. The first thing she had done was to go to Octavia in Ezylryb's hollow. Her mind replayed the scene that had trans-pired there.

"We have a problem." Otulissa had hardly begun to speak when Octavia interrupted her.

"Don't I know it!" the old snake hissed.

"The Striga's been here?" Otulissa was gripped with panic.

"Yes, but he didn't get anything."

"What did he ask for?"

"The legends, the songs, *The History of the Ice Claw Wars, Volumes One and Two*." Octavia was referring to the original manuscripts that Ezylryb had written under the name of Lyze of Kiel. These were locked in a secret compartment in the hollow that few knew about.

Otulissa sighed. "He got the copies of the songs we have in the library and a few other books as well."

"What are you going to do, Otulissa? Confront him?"

"Not yet." Otulissa had thought about this briefly on her way to see Octavia. She feared that this owl, this blue thing, had more followers than she might imagine. Possibly some in the tree, for there were some new owls. But there were always new owls coming to the tree, few to stay, most to study for limited periods of time. But she worried that there might be more followers of the Striga on the mainland. She wasn't sure exactly what he was offering them. But he was undoubtedly a curiosity, exotic, intriguing from his blue feathers to his silky voice with its Jouzhen accent. So Otulissa had bided her time, but she was not perching idly, twiddling her talons. More books were discovered to be missing. She had sneaked into the guest hollow where the Striga was staying one time when she knew he was in deep conversation with Coryn — this growing relationship between Coryn and the Striga worried her to no end — and, while in his hollow, discovered in his fire grate the singed fragments of parchment and paper. A couple of words were still decipherable — "splat," "seagull," "wet." She immediately recognized the pages from the wet poop chapter in *Slightly Filthy Riddles for Soiled Minds* that she had read after the Striga had come into the library and blathered on, praising Otulissa for the practical nature of her work. She recalled his unctuous voice. "Flattery!" The word had exploded in her head as she stood over the scraps of singed paper. It hadn't been praise at all, she realized, but shameless flattery.

Things from that moment on began to fall into place for Otulissa. Had not the Striga himself said, when describing the Dragon Court, that the fuel that fired it was vanity. But that fuel had to be ignited by something, and the kindling of that vanity was flattery delivered every minute of every hour, night in and night out, by the servants. "Oh, good Glaux," Otulissa whispered to herself in a kind of stunned horror, "that is what he was trying to do to me." And, she realized, what he had been doing to Coryn. How clever he was!

It was then in the Striga's hollow when she discovered the burnt scraps of paper that she began to formulate her plan. The first part of it involved removing the most treasured books to a temporary hiding place. One by one, they would move them. The second stage would be transporting them to the Palace of Mists. Hopefully, the Band would return by the time she was back and they could decide how to rid the tree of this dangerous owl.

Otulissa looked up at the stars to check their course, then glanced over at Fritha, who seemed to be flying a bit unevenly. She sensed that the young Pygmy Owl was tiring. Fritha was so fired up about going to the Palace of Mists that Otulissa knew that she would never admit to being tired. Very few owls in the great tree knew about it, even though they owed it much. Fritha, who was smart beyond her years and had suspected another library someplace for a while, was thrilled to be finally going there. She could hardly believe her great luck, although it was a result of a horrendous crime.

Otulissa had confided her plan to only two other owls — Pelli and Bubo. Pelli, it turned out, was very alarmed by what she had heard when Blythe and Bash had reported the activities of the Blue Feather Club. She had been about to insist that Bell return the feather but Otulissa prevailed upon her not to as it might arouse the suspicions of the Striga. Pelli nearly fell off her perch when Otulissa had told her about the book burnings. "Who could have ever imagined! And to think that he was the one who rescued my daughter! What should we do?" Otulissa had said that she must not let on that she was worried to any of her children and, least of all, the Striga.

"You must play this very cool, Pelli. It is the only way we can hope to be safe until the Band is back."

"But Coryn! How could Coryn . . . ?" She hadn't finished the sentence.

All this came back to Otulissa as she flew across the Sea of Hoolemere. "Land ho!" she said, turning to Fritha. The scratchy outline of Cape Glaux appeared on the horizon just as the sky began to lighten. The wind died. The sea grew so still that from the altitude at which they were flying it looked like an enameled surface painted with the first pink streaks of the dawn, twixt time.

CHAPTER TWELVE

A Mist of Gloom

O ne more story, Mum. Please?" Bash begged. It was past First Light and time for all the owls of the great tree to go to sleep. Pelli was exhausted. *I'm this tired,* she thought, *and there has been no real Harvest Festival.* It was amazing how anxiety could just wring every ounce of energy from an owl. She did not want to betray her worry to the young'uns. Earlier that night she had met with Coryn. He had requested that she come to his hollow. In the presence of the Striga he read her a note he had received from the Band saying that they had found it necessary to extend their expedition on the mainland. They had been frustrated in their attempts to track the windkins and needed more time. When she asked if Soren had included a note for her, the Striga answered very quickly that there was no such note. And then rather casually, too casually, he nodded his head and gave a meaningful glance to Coryn.

"You know the Band. They keep to themselves. Often exclude those to whom they owe the most."

"I don't understand what you mean. I am Soren's mate. He would write to me." Pelli did not want to be too pushy. She must play it cool, as Otulissa had cautioned.

"It seems that their first loyalty is always to one another," the Striga said, again with another glance at Coryn.

"I, too, sometimes feel excluded, Pelli," Coryn said sympathetically. Pelli shook her head. It wasn't that she felt excluded. This note from the Band somehow did not feel right to her. She worried about it for the rest of the evening and was still worrying about it as twixt time approached and she was tucking the three B's in for the day.

"Just one more story," Blythe echoed Bash. "I love them so much." Pelli had been reading them some owlet stories based on the legend cycles. They were compelling tales, and Primrose had adapted several for young'uns. Wensel, a very talented young Barn Owl, had illustrated them with quill ink drawings. Pelli noticed that Bell was the only one of her three daughters who had not demanded another. She turned her head to look at the young owl who was feigning sleep, and wondered.

I love them, too, Bell was thinking. *So much, especially the parts about the wolves of the Beyond. But what would the Striga think?* That's what the Striga said they should ask when they were in doubt. They should hold their blue feather close and ask, "What would the Striga think?" But she couldn't reach for her blue feather because then they would know she was not asleep. *Oh, what to do? Does it really hurt me to listen to this?* she wondered. "All right," she heard her mum say. "One more . . ."

Her mother's voice threaded through the milky light that washed into the hollow as the sun rose.

"'In the strange, distant region known as Beyond the Beyond with its clans of dire wolves was one wolf by the name of Fengo, who became a good and great friend of Grank the first collier'. . . ."

By the time their mother finished the story, the young owlets of Pelli and Soren were fast asleep. Pelli retreated to her corner of the hollow and took up a book she had been reading. It was about King Arthur and his knights of the Round Table. Much as Pelli loved the story, she could not concentrate on it. She was worried about Coryn. Since the Band left, he ate alone in his hollow and she had seen him haunting the emptiest branches, gazing into the night sky as if looking for answers. And he was growing thinner. He seemed almost crippled by melancholy. The Others called this condition melancholia, which was far beyond what owls called the gollymopes. Coryn took no joy from life. How could he feel this way here in this magnificent tree on this little piece of Glaux-given earth in the middle of the Hoolemere Sea? Pelli hopped over to the port of the hollow and peered out. Through the shimmering strands of the copper-rose milkberry vines, the daytime world seemed to glow, and beyond the vines she could see patches of the Hoolemere Sea sparkling like jewels. She looked down at the book of legends, which she had left open. There was a magnificent picture of a dire wolf glimmering in a pool of moonlight. That was art, not some proof of vanity. How could Coryn see only sadness and vanity in such a world?

At the same hour of the day that Pelli contemplated the melancholy of Coryn, the young king was alone in his hollow staring fixedly at the spot where the Ember of Hoole had once sat in its teardrop-shaped iron case. It had been so dangerous, having the ember in his hollow. Merely being in the presence of its radiance had made Coryn think strange things. Coryn feared his own vulnerability to the radiance of the ember and often felt unequal to its power. The Band and those close to Coryn had noticed his moodiness around it. Their concern had prompted Otulissa to suggest removing the ember to the ordinary coal pits in Bubo's forge. There, surrounded by other embers, it seemed to be insulated and less able to disturb the owls around it. The whereabouts of the coal was a secret, a deep secret to all but Coryn, Otulissa, the Band, and Bubo, of course. It had been a wonderful solution.

However, in the last few days, the Striga had been pressing Coryn for information about the ember. He had not asked for it directly but he had been very disappointed that Coryn had not been more forthcoming with information.

"I sense," he had said that morning as he visited Coryn in his hollow, "that you are holding something back." Coryn had not replied. "Coryn," he persisted, "there should be no secrets between us."

"Yes, I know," Coryn had said, but did not look straight into those pale eyes from which a stream of weak yellow light flowed. "I feel terrible," Coryn added. But the Striga said nothing. His silence, which seemed to stretch endlessly, made Coryn feel even worse.

Finally, the Striga spoke. "I shall depart this evening on a contemplative journey."

"A scouring one?" Coryn asked.

"Yes, there will be some of that, because it is only when I tear out my own feathers that I can hope to understand this strange impasse at which you and I have arrived."

Coryn felt a deep ache in his gizzard. He groaned. "No," he whispered.

"Coryn," the Striga said patiently. "This will give us both time to reflect. I have failed you in some way. Perhaps away from the great tree and its vanities, I shall gain some insight."

"It's not your fault!" Coryn said almost desperately. But there was no discouraging the blue owl. He left just after tween time. And with each passing hour, Coryn slipped deeper and deeper into a sadness that seemed nearly bottomless. And his sadness seemed contagious. For although during this season of the Copper Rose, the nights had been clear, the stars sharp and brilliant in the sky, and the days bright with sunshine, a gloom seemed to have wrapped itself around the tree like a thin mist. The silence that had prevailed during the Harvest Festival continued. Mysteriously, several strings of the grass harp were broken and had not yet been repaired. So there was no singing or harp guild practice. It was as if life's energy was slowly seeping out of the tree.

CHAPTER THIRTEEN

A World Gone Yoicks?

Although the weather on the Island of Hoole was perfect, with calm seas and flawless skies, such was not the case as one approached the mainland. For several days, cantankerous winds and sudden autumn squalls had buffeted the coastline beyond Cape Glaux and well into the interior. Otulissa and Fritha's flight with the books had taken longer than they had expected. Fritha was tiny even for a Pygmy Owl, but she was an excellent flier and never complained. There was something in this young owl that reminded Otulissa of herself. She possessed a steely determination in the face of difficult odds. At last the two owls had made it to the Palace of Mists and were now perched in the library, exhausted, their botkins deposited on the table. Bess, a Boreal Owl, was helping them unstrap the books from their backs.

"All right, now what is all this about?" Bess asked. She was utterly bewildered. Never had she seen this Spotted

Owl so out of sorts. Otulissa had been thinking how she would explain all of this to her. Bess was strange. Reclusive. She rarely left the Palace of Mists. First and foremost, Bess was a scholar. She had learned the Jouzhen language of the Middle Kingdom and was fairly fluent now. Long before that, she had also learned the language of the Others and enjoyed translating their books for the great tree. But for all her learning, she was not a particularly worldly owl. She lived alone and knew little of the surrounding regions.

Otulissa began: "You know about the blue owl that saved Soren's Bell and alerted us to the slink melf and all that, right?"

"Yes." Bess nodded.

"Well, that same blue owl, who calls himself 'Striga,' or rather 'the Striga,'" Otulissa's facial disk contracted as she said this, and the dark patches that were on either side of her beak seemed to pucker. "The Striga," she repeated, and continued. "Unfortunately, this blue owl is having a bad influence on the tree, especially on Coryn."

"For example?"

"For example, the blue owl is obsessed with what he calls vanities. Excesses, decorations, festivals. There was no Harvest Festival this year."

"Coryn agreed to this?"

Otulissa nodded.

"And why did you bring these books?" Bess said, casting her eyes on the ones that Otulissa and Fritha had just set down. "He claims books are vain?"

Otulissa nodded again, took a step closer, and whispered, "He burns books!"

Bess staggered, blinked, and seemed to have difficulty catching her breath. She had known there had to be a good reason for Otulissa to bring this young Pygmy Owl with her. Otulissa and the Band were sensitive to her reclusive ways.

"Are you all right?" Otulissa said, leaning forward, listening to the Boreal Owl's labored breathing.

"No, I am not all right!" The mist from the great falls against which the palace was built swirled into the library. "Who could be all right on hearing this?" She recovered her breath. "So that is why you brought the books."

"Our most precious ones," Otulissa replied, and then explained how books had begun disappearing from the library, and how she had sneaked into the Striga's hollow and found the burnt scraps of a joke book. "And I am not sure if he is confining his activities to the great tree. I have a feeling that he might actually be doing most of his burning on the mainland. He makes many trips away from the tree for what he calls contemplative journeys or meditative retreats. Since the Great Flourishing more owls read than ever before. More animals of all sorts read. With the press up and running, well, there are simply more books around."

"Around to be burned," Bess said grimly.

"Yes," Otulissa replied.

"This is truly awful." Bess sighed. "Given how I live, the solitary life I pursue, it is not surprising I had not heard of this." She blinked. A horrified light filled her eyes. "Otulissa, it is more important than ever that the Palace of Mists remains a secret." There was a raw desperation in the Boreal Owl's voice.

"Yes," said Otulissa. What, indeed, would happen if the beautiful old stone palace deep in the Shadow Forest was discovered? What then?

Unbeknownst to the Striga when he left the great tree, he had been followed at a very discreet distance by Doc Finebeak. The Snowy was a tracker of great repute and the new mate of Madame Plonk. Doc Finebeak was as angry and upset as he ever had been. The frinkin' blue owl had convinced Coryn to forbid Doc's mate, the magnificent singer of the great tree, to sing. And then shortly after this there was the trouble with the grass harp's strings. When Plonkie, as those closest to her affectionately called her, could not sing, she sank into a terrible spell of the gollymopes. It was just so wrong. He wanted to know what this blue creature — a very poor excuse for an owl in Doc Finebeak's mind — was up to.

So he followed him. The blue owl was a strong flier, given the threadbare condition of his wings. But he was noisy and messy, leaving several clues in his flight track. Doc Finebeak eased himself into the flight groove of the blue owl and followed it right into The Barrens, a treeless landscape due north of Ambala. As with many such landscapes, there were signs of Burrowing Owls. These owls preferred living in ground nests or burrows that they dug with their strong, long, featherless legs. Although the land appeared empty, Finebeak knew there were plenty of places for the Striga to hide. He soon noticed that some other owls had joined the Striga, and he observed that they all sported a single blue feather tucked somewhere into their plumage.

They soon lighted down in an area that Finebeak knew as the "boulder garden." There were many immense boulders that extended for a distance in every direction. Burrowing Owls liked to burrow underneath large rocks and boulders; perhaps it made them feel fortified to have their holes right up against the stone. Doc wasn't sure, but he was able to creep close enough to listen in.

"You say that right here there are offenders?" the blue owl asked one of the others.

"Yes, Striga. Vanities abound."

"I would think that in this barren land, there would be no fripperies or ornamentation."

"It ain't ornamentation so much as books," said a Horned Owl. "Ever since that printing press got started, them books — why, they's like a blight, a disease that's spreading."

"Yes, it spreads," said the blue owl. "I think we need to strike now. Make an example. You say you have a target, an offending burrow?"

"Yes, sir," said a Screech Owl. "Not a quarter league from here and we already found a good pyre."

Pyre, thought Doc Finebeak. *What in hagsmire is a pyre?* He had never heard that word. He felt something crinkle in his gizzard. He suddenly had the most dreadful feeling that a pyre might be a haggish sort of thing. He was crouching behind a bramble of cotton bush. The soft white fuzzy buds opened at this time of the year and provided a perfect camouflage for the Snowy. *What is going on here?* he wondered.

Doc Finebeak would learn all too soon as half a dozen of the twentysome owls gathered rushed into a burrow not far from where Doc was concealed.

"Kalo!!!" An anguished scream split the air. Then pandemonium struck. Owls from nearby burrows poured out. Cries of "It's the Blue Brigade! The Blue Brigade!" came from all sides.

"You were given a warning to turn in your books or be raided," the Striga addressed the crowd. "Prepare to light the pyre."

Now Doc Finebeak saw exactly what a pyre was. How clever! This blue owl and his helpers were using plants that grew here naturally to make a fire. There was a large huckleberry bush and right next to it an immense creosote bush, two of the most combustible plants in the entire Southern Kingdoms. And since there were no trees in this region, there was no threat of forest fires. But still, fire was fire and it could destroy. Finebeak watched in horror as the objects for destruction were ferreted out from the surrounding burrows. The owls of this Blue Brigade came out with scrolls, books, and the occasional sparkly bauble.

"Kalo, let go of it. It's not worth it," Burrowing Owl shouted. "Please, Kalo."

A lovely-looking Burrowing Owl stood in the center of the clearing, clutching a book in her talons. "I just got this book! It *is* worth it," Kalo protested. A Great Horned with a blue feather stuck right between his horn tufts was wrenching the book from her.

"What's the problem here, Field Marshal Cram?" The Striga lighted down.

"Oh, we get one of these book huggers now and again. Won't let go."

"What sort of book is it?" the Striga asked, wondering if it might be a study of something useful like metallurgy and worthy of sparing.

"Looks like a legend of sorts," Cram said.

"Take it away from her," the Striga ordered harshly. "What about fripperies?"

"Some pearls. They look valuable," Field Marshal Cram said, holding up a strand of pink pearls.

"They are!" the owl named Kalo said. "Genuine salt-water pearls. Take them. Just leave me my book!"

"Books, pearls, it makes no difference!" the Great Horned said.

"Let her keep her book," another owl said. He was younger than Kalo, but not young enough to be her son.

"Coryn, stay back," Kalo commanded.

"Did you say 'Coryn'?!" The blue owl wilfed, as did his companions.

"Yes," replied Kalo. "Although sometimes we call him Cory." Planting her long, slender, featherless legs in the ground, she drew herself up to her full height, which was impressive. "My brother was named for our king." The nearly horizontal band of white feathers across the top of her brown head framed her yellow eyes, giving them a powerful intensity. Doc was impressed with this Kalo. She could certainly stand up to a threat.

"That's blasphemy — using the name of our revered king," the Striga spat.

"I knew the king when he was but a lad and I was a lass. We were both young'uns." A quiet had settled on the owls. "When he was not a king but an outcast." Kalo extended her wing and gently touched her brother's shoulder with the tip. "He saved my mother's egg. And from that egg came Coryn."

"Da, what is happening to Mummy?" a little hatchling screeched from where she crouched between her father's legs.

"Hush, Siv," Kalo said.

"Siv?" The blue owl blinked. "I've heard that name. Who is she?"

"A queen. A queen from long, long ago in the time of the legends and these are her stories." Kalo was standing on one leg, balancing perfectly as Burrowing Owls could, and with her other talon she clutched to her breast the book entitled *Siv, a Queen's Tale*.

Doc blinked away tears. This was some owl, this Kalo!

The Striga opened his beak wide and cried out, "Ignite!" There was a great explosion and the creosote bush erupted into a ball of fire. The Striga ripped the book from Kalo's talons.

"Who ordered this . . . this insanity?" Kalo cried above the roar of the flames.

"Your precious king, madam, your precious king!" the Striga said.

What! Doc Finebeak thought. *Has the entire world gone yoicks?* And as if to confirm this, he heard a triumphant, maniacal hooting overhead. A formation of owls from the Blue Brigade was flying over the pyre. Each owl carried a book and dropped it into the fire. The flames seemed to reach up for the books, craving them, thirsting for them, and as each book dropped, the fire raged more fiercely. Random white pages fluttered up like scorched doves, the edges of their wings turning black and curling up until the page was consumed and disintegrated into a swirl of ash.

Doc Finebeak observed it all. He could not tear his eyes away, he felt that he should not. There must be a witness to this horror. His gizzard was in turmoil as he noted every sickening little detail. Just before a book caught the flames, when it was still fresh to the fire, it was seized with a series of odd little movements. Its pages, stirred by the heated wind, began to turn by themselves. The glue in the spines burbled and thin tendrils of dark smoke rose. And finally the edges of the pages darkened to amber. The amber turned to black, and then the book consumed itself. Some books, perhaps newer ones in which the glue was fresher, simply exploded.

Doc Finebeak finally turned his gaze from the fire and looked in a mixture of horror and curiosity upon the face of the Striga. Nearly featherless now, the puckered skin was bathed in the shifting orange light of the flames. His yellow eyes glimmered and his beak hung open as he watched, transfixed by the terrible beauty of this forest of flames.

"He's mad," Doc Finebeak murmured. *I must take Plonkie far away, as far away as possible,* he thought. *Maybe to the Northern Kingdoms, who knows? She could become a gadfeather. Those are her roots.* And the Snowy knew that if they were burning books now, what would be next, owls? And the first owls to be burned would probably be artists, great artists like Madame Plonk, the love of his life.

CHAPTER FOURTEEN
Mists of Ambala

I was expecting you," came the familiar voice.

The vaporous scarves of swirling mist that had seconds before seemed so random sorted themselves into spots, patches of light and dark, and gradually into a shape, a shape not unlike that of a Spotted Owl. Before them, perched on the edge of the huge eagle's nest, was the elusive, ethereal owl known as Mist by most, except for a very few who called her by her original name, Hortense.

"Hortense," Soren blurted out. Gylfie and Soren had come to know her years before when they were both imprisoned in St. Aggie's.

A glimmer shivered through the vapors. "Ooooh!" Hortense said. "It's so nice to hear my real name. You know, no one calls me that anymore and yet there are all these little Hortenses flying about in Ambala."

It was true, of course, that in Ambala the name Hortense was the most popular for either girl or boy hatchlings. There was a saying in Ambala that a hero was known by only one name and that name was Hortense. Before the Pure Ones, St. Aggie's had wreaked terror and havoc on the Southern Kingdoms, owl-napping hatchlings and even eggs from nests. In that time, Hortense had infiltrated St. Aggie's, posing as a young defenseless owl. She had succeeded in penetrating the eggorium and, with the help of two bald eagles, rescued countless eggs. As Hortense grew older, however, she seemed to grow dimmer, almost fading away. She attributed this to the large deposits of flecks in the streams and soil of Ambala, which she said could change the nature of an owl born there, proving to be either a blessing or a curse. But the Band had never seen another owl in Ambala that resembled this mysterious owl. She was a legend, but for the Band, in particular Soren and Gylfie, she was very real. Her presence was as compelling as it ever was.

"So you knew we were coming, Hortense?" Gylfie asked.

Always one to cut to the chase, Hortense replied, "It's about the book burnings, isn't it, and these Blue Brigades?" In that moment, two massive eagles plummeted out of the sky and landed on the opposite side of the immense nest. They were accompanied by two flying snakes.

"You said they'd come." Streak, the smaller of the two eagles, spoke. His mate, Zan, was mute and merely nodded. Her tongue had been ripped out some years before in a brutal battle with the St. Aggie's forces. "The book burnings, eh?"

Soren just shook his head. "We had no idea it was this widespread. We saw one, but that was way up in Silverveil, near the notch."

"That's where most of them have been," Streak said. "But just now we saw a huge fire over in The Barrens."

Then the two luminous bright green snakes hissed. Even after having met them on many occasions each one of the Band wilfed slightly upon seeing these two snakes. There was nothing quite like the flying snakes of Ambala. They possessed one of the deadliest venoms on Earth which, when used correctly, could cure instead of kill. Twilight's life had been saved by these snakes when he had sustained what everyone thought was a mortal wound in battle. Now both Slynella and her mate, Stingyll, were hissing in an absolute fury. "And to think," the words always seemed to slither off their tongue, "we were the ones to teach him how to read," Stingyll said.

"Yesssss," agreed Slynella. "It sssseemss ssso long ago. What happened?"

"What are you talking about?" Digger asked.

"The book burningsss," Stingyll said.

"You taught the blue owl how to read?" Soren asked.

"No, no, never!" Slynella gave a scorching hiss. "Coryn . . . Coryn, when he was ssstill called Nyroc. We ssspelled out his name for him, like thisss, through our sssky writing." Slynella immediately flew off the edge of the nest into the air, and Stingyll followed. They began scrolling themselves into myriad shapes and gradually letters began to form. "You sssee, it wasss all his idea. To reverse the ssspelling of his original name from Nyroc to Coryn!" Slynella paused. "That owl'sss a geniussss!"

"Yesss. Ssso why isss he ssso dumb now?" Stingyll asked.

The Band was bewildered. Soren flew straight up to them as they continued to slither out in midair. "It's the Striga that is burning books. What does any of this book burning have to do with Coryn?"

"Why, he ordered it," Slynella said. "The Ssstriga is acting on Coryn's command."

Soren felt himself wilf. Zan, the larger of the eagles, flew to him instantly.

"She's got you, Soren. She's got you," Hortense called out.

"I'm fine, don't worry." But, indeed, Soren had started to go yeep.

The entire Band was stunned by this news. "I just simply can't believe it." Gylfie shook her head. "We all know that Coryn has been growing very close to the Striga, but I never thought he'd have that much influence."

"Well, we came here for information and we got it," Twilight said, looking across the eagle's nest at Hortense, who was hovering near Streak.

"But what are we to do?" Soren asked. "This is not exactly war."

"It could be," Twilight said.

"But right now, it's about books," Soren said.

"Books and owls," Hortense said. "This Striga and his Blue Brigade have been raiding nests, hollows, burrows, looking for books and the things they call vanities — ripping apart owl homes." The mist around Hortense seemed to quiver almost sadly. She continued, "There are rumors that a few from the great tree's library were stolen right from under the librarian's nose and brought to the mainland and burned."

"No!" The four owls of the Band all wilfed.

"That sounds like war to me," Twilight said.

"But the question, Twilight," the vapors shimmered a bit as Hortense turned toward the Great Gray, "the question is, how do you proceed if it is war?" Twilight started to answer, but Soren put out his wing and touched him lightly, a silent signal to wait, to listen, which was not first nature to Twilight. But Soren knew that Hortense was a subtle thinker. He wanted to hear her thoughts on this. "I don't think it has come to war yet. The blue owl lives at the great tree, and is a close advisor to your king. Do you attack the tree? I think not. First, you must save the books before it is too late, and then stop this terrible destruction of art, the fripperies, as he calls anything pretty." She looked at the Great Gray. "You see, Twilight, knowledge is more than equivalent to force." Hortense paused. "I read that in a scrap from the *Fragmentum*, a part of a book by an Other named Doctor Sam. I began thinking about knowledge as force, and books as important as battle claws."

"She's got to be kidding!" Twilight muttered.

Soren gave him a swift kick. "Go on," Soren urged.

"I have started a program here in Ambala."

"A program," Twilight said with more than a tinge of despair in his voice.

"Yes. You see we have been fearful of this for some time now and have established a place in Ambala that we call the Place of Living Books."

"Tell us about it," Digger said.

Hortense shimmered a bit as the beads of mist seemed to thicken, then re-sort themselves. "Since the printing press was built and began working the owls of Ambala have become passionate readers and book lovers. But not many books come our way. I think it is the lingering suspicions many owls still have of the flecks in our streams. Let's just say we are sort of 'back woods,' not along the usual well-worn flight paths. Even Mags doesn't venture here often. But the few books that come our way, we treasure. So when we began to hear about the book burnings, we wanted to do whatever we could to protect our books."

"So what did you do?" Twilight asked. "What is this Place of Living Books?"

"Well, I cannot take all the credit, really. A young Whiskered Screech named Braithe thought up the idea. We could go there tonight, if you like, but there is not much left of this night and the distance is far. And you know I am a weak flier," Hortense added.

Thus, the owls settled down into the immense aerie on the highest peak in Ambala. Silvery clouds scraped across the last remnants of the night. The snakes twined themselves through the branches of the aerie and glimmered in the rising sun like bright ribbons. They would keep the day watch, for their sleeping habits were very different from those of owls.

Had they, however, kept a night watch and not frolicked so heartily performing their skywriting, they might have caught sight of a Burrowing Owl hiding in one of the thick cumulus clouds. Concealed under his coverts was a small blue feather. He was a spy and what he had seen was strange, very strange. But he knew it was good information, valuable information. He did not particularly like wearing the stupid blue feather, but compromises had to be made. He would be handsomely rewarded. One had to look out for one's own self-interests, after all, and his future was uncertain since that last battle in the Middle Kingdom.

CHAPTER FIFTEEN
Word by Word

"This can't be so, can it, Mrs. Plithiver?"

"I'm afraid it is." Soren peeked into his hollow. Pelli was sobbing.

"Why? Why would he abandon us like this?" she was saying. "Why have they all left?"

"But I haven't!" Soren exclaimed. "I am right here. Right here! Can't you see me?" He flew into the hollow and alighted on his old perch, the one from which he often read to the three B's. But Pelli and the three B's stared right through him. Was it possible? Had he become like mist, some vaporous collection of insignificant water droplets in the air? His gizzard froze. "It's me!" he cried out to them. "Me!"

"Wake up, Soren, You're dreaming. Just dreaming," Gylfie said, fluttering above her best friend. Her tiny wings beat madly in an attempt to fan him and bring Soren out of whatever terrible dream he was lost in.

"But it was so real!" Soren gasped.

"It was just a dream," Gylfie said again. Digger and Twilight exchanged nervous glances. They all knew that for Soren there was no such thing as just a dream. Soren possessed a rare ability: starsight, which was a kind of dream vision in which he could see the future, or things that were happening in some distant place. The other members of the Band never asked him for the details of these visions. There was a silent understanding that it was best not to make such inquiries.

"Look," said Digger, trying to quell any telltale quaver in his voice. "It's almost tween time." The sky was streaked with the deep purples of twilight. In another few minutes it would be completely black. "What do you say we get going to this book place?"

"What, no tweener? I'm starved," Twilight said.

"I prefer to fly light," Hortense said. It was all the Band could do to keep from bursting out in churrs of laughter. Light? What could be lighter than Hortense, who was not much more than a collection of dewdrops? "Don't worry, Twilight," Hortense added. "We'll pass over a meadow that is crawling with voles. You can eat on the fly." Eating on the fly was a skill that all Guardians had developed to a high degree, especially in time of war. It involved seizing the prey, then immediately taking off again and dismembering it to be shared as they flew.

They found a plump summer vole almost immedi-ately. "Can't believe how much fat this fellow still has on him," Twilight said. "And here we are well into autumn."

"He must have been lounging around in his hole," Gylfie said.

"Must have been a tight fit for a chubby rodent like this," Digger commented.

They all churred. Digger, being a Burrowing Owl and superb excavator for the construction of nesting burrows, was an expert in such matters.

"I'll just take the tongue," Hortense said.

"You sure?" Soren asked.

"Oh, yes. Fatty foods, yechhh! Just can't eat them any-more." Once again the Band was struck by the oddity of Hortense's remarks on eating.

With his superb hearing, Soren could pick up all of the squeaks and grunts and grinds of their gizzards as they digested the bones and hair of the vole, organizing it into the tight packets that would soon be pellets. It seemed deafening to him. He flew off from the others for he wanted to be able to hear the first sounds of this Place of Living Books.

Hortense was soon beside him. Her own gizzard was almost perfectly silent. Whatever mechanisms turned there were closer to the sounds of the fluttering wings of a moth than a gizzard packing pellets.

"You won't hear anything, Soren, until we're actually there," Hortense said.

"Really?"

"Yes, you see, Braithe, who is somewhat of a genius, chose this place carefully. It's what we used to call the moss hole. There's a deep dip in this part of the forest, and the steep sides of it are lined with the thickest moss that you've ever seen. It absorbs every bit of sound."

"You said you used to call it the moss hole. What do you call it now?"

"The Brad," Hortense replied.

"The Brad?" Soren asked.

"Braithe will explain." Hortense paused, just a beat. "All will be revealed."

And, indeed, word by word, all began to be revealed. As they flew, the verdant landscape below them suddenly pitched steeply into a small valley.

"Are those the crowns of heartwoods?" Digger asked, pointing to the lush, dense canopy that capped the steep dell. "They don't seem tall enough to be heartwood trees."

"Oh, they are," Mist replied. Heartwood trees grew to enormous heights. Had the grove of trees not been rooted deep in the moss-lined dell, their lush crowns would have scratched the sky, towering above the surrounding trees. They were the only species that even came close to the Great Ga'Hoole Tree in size. Hortense now began a steep banking turn, and they followed her, losing altitude. As they drew closer to the trees, the dell appeared to widen. They could now see that the heartwoods were clustered in a dense grove in the bottom of a mossy bowl-like valley. As they spiraled into this bowl, the light changed. It seemed to glow with a dim shimmering amber radiance. They caught the sweet scent of mint on the light breezes that found their way into the bowl. It did seem to be a place of enchantment.

The Band swung their heads in wonder as they perched on something as puffed and cushiony as one of the velvet pillows from Trader Mags' "interior collection," as she called it. But it wasn't a pillow or a cushion. It was a moss-covered rock. Hortense's remarks about the moss were understated to say the least. Nothing could have prepared them for this thickly lined green place, so hidden, so insulated from the world around them that it might as well have been in the stars. And walking, perched, or flying in low orbits were two dozen or more owls. Words, countless words flowed from their beaks. An Elf Owl swooped by:

"'Call me Grank. I am an old owl now as I set down these words but this story must be told, or at least begun before I pass on. Times are different now than they were when I was young. I was born into a time of chaos and everlasting wars.'"

The Band blinked and looked at one another in wonder. It was the first volume of the legends cycle, the story of the first collier.

"Amazing!" Digger said in a hushed voice. And at just that moment a burly Great Horned flew by. In a deep-throated voice that was almost a growl he recited:

"'What were my feelings that night as I huddled with my faithful servant, Myrrthe, the Great Snowy, both of us trying to protect the egg that would be my first child if it was not seized by the hagsfiends? Though a queen, I do not think that my feelings were different from those of any other mother. . . .'"

It did not sound the least bit odd to hear this deep male voice with a rough burr on its edges intoning *The Queen's Tale*. This slim volume, the story of Queen Siv, the mother of Hoole, had been found recently, preserved intact in a niche deep in the Ice Cliff Palace where Siv had hidden for a while during the terrible wars nearly a thousand years before.

Hortense seemed to be glimmering with a new intensity. "This is the Place of Living Books. Nowhere in all the owl kingdoms do I think books are as treasured as they are here in Ambala." She shook her head and the vaporous drops seemed to blur for an instant. "I don't know why. Blame it on the flecks!" She churred. "But each of these owls has devoted his or her life to memorizing at least one book, word by word, and passages of others." A Snowy Owl now swept by, and Soren gasped as he caught the first words.

> "'It befell in the days of Uther Pendragon, when he was king of all England, and so reigned, that there was a mighty duke in Cornwall and he was called the duke of Tintagel and it was at this castle of Tintagel that Arthur was born of Igraine.'"

The Snowy was reciting the legends of King Arthur. This was one of his and Pelli's favorite of all the Others' books, even dearer to them than the Shakes plays. Soren thought again about what he had glimpsed in the torn fabric of his dream. His dear Pelli not recognizing him. It was too much for Soren.

"Ah, there's Braithe!" Hortense waved one of her stubby wings.

The Whiskered Screech ceased his recitation and landed on a stump beside the rock where they were perched. He looked incredibly young to the Band.

"So you're the young'un who organized all this," Gylfie said.

"I love to read, that's all," the young Screech replied.

"He's very modest," Hortense offered. "Explain to my friends about this place and why we now call it the Brad."

"Well." Braithe sighed. "When the reports of these book burnings came in, our first thoughts were to hide the books. But then I thought better. Yes, we could hide the books, but what if they were found? Then what?"

The four owls of the Band blinked at each other.

"Precisely." Braithe continued, "But what if each owl who loved to read *became* a book? Memorized every word on every page." He paused. "That's just what we did. Think of each of us as not a collection of feathers but book covers." He puffed up his beautiful plumage. He was a handsome tawny gray with a generous sprinkling of white in his coverts. He looked in that instant so much like Ezylryb that it almost took the Band's breath away. But they said nothing. "The idea is not mine. Not at all. You see, I was inspired. My inspiration is, or rather was, an Other."

"An Other?" they all gasped.

"Yes, a writer I discovered when the first volume of the *Fragmentum* was completed. Only scraps of his writings were found — wherever it is that they find these things." The Band exchanged nervous looks. It was more important than ever that the whereabouts of the Palace of Mists be kept a secret.

Braithe continued, "The author's full name is not known. We call him Ray Brad. We think it's only scraps of his name but what is important is that he wrote about book burning. I think the Others went through a time similar to ours. To save their books, the Others began to memorize them. So that is how I got the idea. And that is why we call this place the Brad. It is the Place of Living Books, named for a dead author."

"A dead species," Twilight added.

Gylfie closed her eyes. "Twilight!" She was mortified. How did the Great Gray just come out with these things at such inappropriate moments?

"Extinct," Digger said quietly.

"Well, gone is gone," Twilight grumped.

"But you see, that's just the point." Braithe spoke with a new intensity. "Ray Brad isn't gone. At least not completely. His work remains, right here!" He raised his foot and tapped his handsome head with a talon. "And here." He tapped his talon now lightly on his belly indicating roughly the spot of his gizzard.

"So welcome to the Brad. The books shall survive!" Braithe spread his wings and flew off. The Band strained to hear the words he was reciting, but fog swirled down into the Brad, and Braithe seemed to be swallowed by its vapors.

For Soren, the entire world suddenly felt very fragile. Did Digger, Gylfie, and Twilight feel this way, too? He must get back to the great tree. Punkie Night was just a short time off. The moon was almost full again. They had been gone for nearly an entire moon cycle. And what had they accomplished with their weather experiments? Practically nothing. But what had they seen? Something that they could have never imagined — the burning of books, a violation that struck at the very gizzard of the principles of the great tree, ordered by its king!

CHAPTER SIXTEEN

This Is Hagscraft!

Scroom, you say?" The Striga thrust his puckered face closer to Tarn, the Burrowing Owl. "You saw those four consorting with a scroom in Ambala?"

"Yes, high in an aerie where two eagles live."

"Did you follow them any farther?"

"No, sir. They rested there for the day. I felt I should report to you as quickly as possible. Your wisdom, your profound insights . . ."

But the Striga cut him off. "Don't flatter me!" he said sharply. The Striga was an expert in matters of flattery, adept with fawning, honeyed words. But he felt a deadly squirm in his gizzard when he was on the receiving end of such blandishments and adulation. For he knew that the core of all flattery was deceit. This Tarn was smart. He would have to watch him. However, he did not know that much about him. He came from some place in the Desert of Kuneer. There had been rumors of some owls holing up there, but he had no time to think about that now. He wanted to reflect on this fresh bit of news. He could not have hoped for better. He must think very carefully on how to make the best use of it. It could be the initial move in dislodging the Band from the great tree and might lead to their ultimate downfall. *Careful, careful,* he admonished himself. He then turned his head and peered with his pale yellow eyes that appeared to Tarn like watered egg yolks. "Thank you. You have served well, efficiently. Your skills are valued." *Now that,* he thought, *is how to discreetly flatter an owl.* The little speech was a model of sincerity and yet not excessive. But it would gain this owl's trust faster than any overly sweet words. Oh, he would sweeten it up as time went on. But there was a course to these things, a pace as well. "Now, please leave me. I must think on this disturbing news."

I will break this news to the great tree, he thought. *But when the time is right. After Punkie Night! Yes, of course Punkie Night. They are all so sure it will be cancelled. They will be thrilled when Coryn says it won't be....* But then he had another thought. The Band might be back by Punkie Night. Although it was mainly a favorite among young owls, older owls donned masks as well, and it was said that Twilight loved this night more than any other. That presented a problem. But then again the masks would provide the perfect cover for the Blue Brigade. They could be at the tree, masked, in substantial numbers without arousing suspicion.

Finally, a complete plan came to him. The word must go out here on the mainland of the Band's heinous treachery — consorting with scrooms, conjuring up the dead, dabbling in hagscraft! The news must be spread that they were no longer welcome at the tree. No — better yet: A rumor that they have gone to serve in the Northern Kingdoms, deserted the tree! Broken their Guardian oath! They can be effectively exiled, as conjurers and traitors! He could make it work, he knew it. It was less than a week to Punkie Night. When he had left the tree, some owls were already busy with the preparations. He would send back a message to Coryn that it was indeed time for a celebration. Punkie Night must go on. Madame Plonk must sing. If they were busy preparing for this stupid holiday, they would be nicely distracted. But in the meantime, he would make sure that here on the mainland the word went out. There were two ways to spread that information. He would use both. The first way was grog trees, and the second was scribes. He would send the Blue Brigade to the grog trees — without their telltale blue feathers — to talk and begin the rumors of the Band's perfidy. The second method was scribes. The number of owls who could be hired to write for those

who were still illiterate, or post public notices throughout the kingdoms had increased dramatically on the
mainland in recent years. He would use them. But first, he
must get word back to the tree about Punkie Night.

Just before dawn, the messenger arrived and was ush-
ered into Coryn's hollow. The young king was still
wondering if he had so gravely offended the Striga that he
would not return. Coryn had been in turmoil since the
Striga's departure. Here, the very owl to whom they owed
their existence because of his valorous, selfless acts had
been driven from the tree perhaps forever because of
Coryn's own stubbornness.

He dismissed the messenger so he could read the message in complete privacy.

Dear Coryn,

*I have been thinking a lot about our last discussion and I under-
stand your fears concerning the ember. But Coryn, you underestimate
your own strengths. You are more than able to withstand the ember's
so-called bad influences. Everywhere I go on the mainland, I see evidence of your own powers as king. The spread of culture, practical
culture, the kind that I approve of, that will add to the betterment of
our world, is amazing. You are an owl of unparalleled courage and
intelligence, with a natural instinct for leadership. I have heard of
your ancient King Hoole, but I believe you shall far exceed him. I*

now think that in many ways I have been too harsh. It was an act of great sacrifice on your part to give up the Harvest Festival. Therefore, with that in mind and upon great reflection, I believe that Punkie Night should go forward. It is a harmless celebration, mostly enjoyed by the young. So, please go on with the celebration. I shall be back by Punkie Eve if not before.

Yours in faith,

Striga

Coryn was so relieved, so happy he thought he might cry. He read the letter twice over, and then went out immediately to make the announcement. Oh, there would be a Punkie Night as never before!

It had been two nights since the Band had left Ambala. They had long forgotten the weather experiments, the original reason for their trip to the mainland. They were much more interested in trying to determine how widespread the influence of the Striga and his Blue Brigade were. To do this they had to operate with some stealth. Keep a low wing, flying on the edges of the night. There was always the chance of being mobbed by crows, but in recent times, ever since Doc Finebeak, a great friend of crows, had begun to reside at the tree, the Guardians had been mostly left alone by the raucous creatures. Therefore, more and more the Band found their flights extending into the morning and even afternoon hours of the day. Unfortunately, they came across ample evidence of the Blue Brigade's devastation. They spotted numerous smoldering fires each morning, littered with the charred remnants of ornaments obviously bought from Trader Mags: countless books, scorched jewels, singed scraps of paintings.

One evening shortly after leaving Ambala, a piece of paper flapping against a slender birch tree attracted their attention. They flew down to take a closer look.

"What the . . ." Gylfie reached it first and was hovering as she read it aloud.

"'*The four members of the Guardians of the Great Ga'Hoole Tree, known collectively throughout the owl kingdoms as the Band, were seen consorting with scrooms and dabbling in faithless acts of hagscraft. They were doing this under the cover of a so-called scientific expedition. Further information suggests that they have renounced their Guardian oath and switched their allegiance to the Northern Kingdoms. For this reason, the parliament of the Great Ga'Hoole Tree forbids anyone to welcome them into their hollows, speak to them, or transact any manner of business with them. Warning: These owls are considered dangerous.'*"

Luckily, the ground was only a foot or so beneath them because Gylfie, Digger, and Soren looked at each other, wilfed, and went yeep, falling gently to the ground.

"This is outrageous!" Soren shouted.

"We're as good as exiled," Digger said.

"Twilight, get over here!" Soren yelled. "You gotta look at this notice written by some scribe. Absolutely outrageous!"

Gylfie turned her head to look at Twilight, who had been investigating a still smoldering fire. The Great Gray looked like a pillar of solid ashes. He was frozen, stiff, like one of the statues in the Palace of Mists.

What could have silenced Twilight? They all rushed over to where the Great Gray stood and looked down.

There was the charred skeleton of an owl, still lashed to the stump of a burnt stake.

"This is hagscraft!" Soren said in a hoarse whisper.

CHAPTER SEVENTEEN
The Wing Prints of Bao

Far away, across a vast sea at the end of the River of Wind, a blue owl perched. Tengshu had been the sage of these Luminous Pearl Gates at the river's end for years beyond counting. Perched on his branch of meditation, he looked out toward the River of Wind where the qui he flew danced in the patchwork of gusts.

Tengshu flew his qui for many reasons. Often for the sheer joy of it, and at other times to collect vital weather information about the air currents, wind speeds, and any shifts in the windkin. But he also flew them when he needed to meditate on a question, and at this moment, Tengshu was deeply disturbed and needed to meditate. He sensed that things were not as they should be in the Hoolian world. In particular, he was worried about his good friends, the four owls known as the Band. He knew that the blue owl, the one who had renamed himself "the Striga," had never returned to the Dragon Court. He had gone missing shortly after the battle at the owlery.

He had distinguished himself at this battle not so much for his courage but for the brutality with which he had killed. This went against every tenet of Danyar, the way of noble gentleness. The Hoolian owls had said that he could return with them, and Tengshu had concluded that, in fact, the former Dragon Court owl had flown to the five kingdoms of the Hoolian world.

Accompanying this certainty, another feeling had been building in him, and it was that the Band in particular, and consequently the great tree, was in some sort of peril. It was just a feeling. He had no evidence as he had for the dragon owl's flight, but his uneasiness had been growing steadily. He had never traveled to the Hoolian kingdoms, but his mother had done so hundreds of years before. As the qui dong of the Luminous Pearl Gates, it was his job to welcome any owls who found their way across the River of Wind. Very few ever had. He led a very reclusive life, one of contemplation. He pursued his poetry and his painting and, when called upon, he could fight. But this was seldom. He realized now, however, as the sun broke over the low clouds, that he must act soon. It suddenly became clear to Tengshu that he could not meditate, equivocate a moment longer. He must go. To remain a recluse at times like these was a terrible self-indulgence. He thought of his mother, Bao. She had made this same trip for reasons he had not completely understood at the time. She had gone without a minute's hesitation. His father had been left to care for Tenghsu and his siblings. *Enough of this!* he thought to himself. Without another second wasted, Tengshu spread his wings and lifted into flight. Following the qui lines to the windkins, he effortlessly soared over them and joined that spectacular and boisterous river of wind. *In my mother's wing prints,* he thought. *The wing prints of Bao!*

CHAPTER EIGHTEEN

The Imperiled Ember

Punkie Night had arrived. Everyone was overjoyed that this night that had been celebrated for countless years had not been cancelled as the Harvest Festival had been. The mood of the tree had lightened considerably. Many concessions had been made for the evening's entertainment. Madame Plonk had been permitted to sing as she always had on Punkie Night in her fabulous gadfeather costume. Pelli was watching from the gallery in the Great Hollow as Madame Plonk began yet another wonderful ballad. Doc Finebeak was looking upon his mate rapturously. Despite his misgivings and his decision to leave, he felt it would be unfair to deny Plonkie this chance to sing. He had not told her yet that he thought they should leave immediately after Punkie Night. Pelli herself was relieved. She sensed that Finebeak was so distressed over his mate's silencing by Coryn that he had been considering leaving the great tree. He had said to Pelli that he had something he must speak to her about, but after Punkie Night.

Madame Plonk was singing a very old ballad from the Northern Kingdoms. Doc Finebeak's gizzard trembled, for the song his mate sang was portentous to say the least.

> *Fly away with me,*
> *Give my loneliness a break.*
> *Fly away with me,*
> *So my heart will never ache.*
> *Fly away with me this night.*
> *Fly away with me.*

Would she have really left? Pelli wondered. *What a loss!* Then, suddenly, something caught her eye. She wasn't sure what. A gesture of some sort from the blue owl? How he had bent his head toward Coryn as he whispered to him? Her hearing was as fine as any Barn Owl's. What was it? She began to observe more closely the Striga and Coryn as Madame Plonk's magnificent voice swelled into the Great Hollow with the accompaniment of the newly repaired grass harp plucked by the nest-maid snakes of the harp guild. There was no doubt about it, the Striga was uncomfortable with this extravagant display of what he must have felt were dangerous vanities. She also watched Coryn, who seemed to be furtively glancing at the Striga as if taking his measure. Coryn, she could tell, was extremely worried. Not worried about the tree, nor about the owls who seemed finally to be lifting out of the depressed mood that had enveloped the tree since the Harvest Festival. *No*, Pelli thought with sharp alarm. *He's worried about the Striga!* Then it came to her with great clarity. *He's made a deal with the Striga. Let us have Punkie Night and then . . . and then what? What did the Striga demand in return?* The very question sent a chill through her gizzard. The ember! She was certain: The ember was in danger. She had to find Bubo immediately. But how? Everyone was wearing masks. Owls were so starved for celebrations that even the older ones who never dressed up were all wearing masks. How would she ever figure out which one was Bubo?

Frantically, she spun her head around, scanning the gallery for Bubo. There was a Great Horned nearby in the mask of a Spotted Owl with a cloak of spotted feathers, but his own shown through. Pelli flew up to him and peered directly in his face.

"I beg your pardon, madam!" the owl replied coolly at her sudden intrusion. He was speaking with a Burrowing Owl.

"Oh, sorry," Pelli apologized. "I thought you were someone else." She had never seen either one of these owls at the tree before. But it was not unheard of for strangers to come from the mainland for the various celebrations. Although there did seem to be an awful lot of them tonight. But where was Bubo? The harp guild snakes had started to pluck a jig, and there were owls fly-dancing outside the tree. She would have a look.

A quarter of an hour later, she had still not found him. Back inside she went. A flash of ruddy feathers peeking out from under a cape of snowy-white ones caught her eye, and then there were his horns barely concealed under the white mask. It was Bubo, she was sure, and he was weaving about in slow glaucana, a kind of waltz, with Otulissa. *Great!* Pelli thought. They both needed to know about her terrible gizzard-wrenching feelings. Otulissa was wearing the mask of a Great Gray but she was unmistakable. She was a lovely fly-dancer, much better really than Bubo. She danced with great style, a crisp yet fluid motion.

"I need to see both of you right now!" Pelli hissed. Mrs. Plithiver, who was just wending her way as a sliptween through an octave, swung her head in the direction of Pelli. She sensed a thin filament of tension in the air. It was pronounced, because all of the other owls for the first time in a long while seemed to be relaxed and enjoying the celebration.

Bubo and Otulissa immediately sensed the rising panic in Pelli's voice. "Where should we meet?"

"The forge," Pelli replied. "But leave separately and by different ports. I'll take an interior corridor. They will just think I'm tired and going to my hollow."

They. The word sounded ominous to Otulissa. She glanced over at the Striga and Coryn.

Pelli actually got to Bubo's forge first. When the two other owls entered, they saw her peering into the coal pits where he kept his bonk embers. Immediately, they knew what she wanted. "The ember is in danger, isn't it?" Otulissa blurted out.

"I knew this celebration stuff was too good to last." Bubo sighed, pulling off his Snowy Owl mask and cloak.

"It just came to me. I don't know how. I was looking at Coryn and the Striga when I had a feeling deep in my gizzard and suddenly realized that Coryn has weakened in some terrible way, that he's going to come for the ember. I know it."

"So, what do we do?" Bubo asked.

Pelli's dark eyes shone with such a luster that had she been outside and not in the cave, they would have reflected the moon and the stars. "We get it out of here. We substitute another."

"A substitute?" Bubo said with a note of incredulity in his voice. "Won't he know?"

Otulissa swiveled her head and peered with her amber eyes into Pelli's dark ones. "You think Coryn has been weakened to the point where he won't notice the difference, right?"

"Possibly." Pelli nodded.

"You think or you hope?" Otulissa asked pointedly.

Pelli sighed. "A little bit of both, I suppose. But what do we have to lose?"

Otulissa knew that Pelli was right. What did they have to lose? At the very least, the ember would be safely tucked away someplace. Otulissa now turned to Bubo. "Do you have a bonk coal that is a reasonable facsimile?"

"Reasonable facsimile of the Ember of Hoole?" Bubo raised a talon to his head and scratched between his horn tufts. "Not likely, but I suppose I could try to fire-juice one." Fire-juicing was a way of heating coals so that their interior structure changed slightly to radiate a more intense heat for a short period of time.

Bubo was now poking around in one of the coal pits. With his tongs, he plucked out an ember. "Here she be." The tongs pinched a glowing coal. Deep in the ember's gizzard, there was a lick of blue and around it a pulsating ring of green. The air seemed to tingle as Bubo held it up. Each one of them could feel it. Dislodged from the other embers in the pit, its power was more direct. It was amazing that Bubo himself had been able to live with it and suffer no ill effects. But he was a blacksmith. He had built up his resistance to it, and it had been buried with other coals, which had acted as a shield. "You see, it's that green that is hard to reproduce. It truly is the color of the wolves' eyes." Bubo was talking about the great dire wolves of the Beyond, who for centuries had guarded the ember as it nestled in its lava cocoon in the volcano called Hrath'ghar. "But you never can tell, Coryn might not notice."

"Right now we have to get the real ember out of here," Otulissa said. "Where do you think you should take it?"

"The Palace of Mists," Pelli answered.

Otulissa closed her eyes. She had suspected that Pelli might say this. Pelli had never been there. Bess would not like it. Otulissa could go, but she had made so many trips already with Fritha transporting books that she was worried about arousing the Striga's suspicions. Pelli was a strong flier and very fast and if she left immediately, she might not be missed.

"All right, I'll give you the navigational coordinates. You're going to have to leave immediately. In the meantime, Bubo, start juicing another coal to substitute for the Ember of Hoole."

"I already got me eye on one down there. But understand that when Pelli flies with this ember, we have to put it in a good strong botkin with some other bonk ones to insulate her from its power."

"And do you have the case, the original one that we always kept it in?"

"Yeah, it's around here someplace."

"Well, you better be prepared. Coryn might come asking for it anytime." Otulissa felt her gizzard twitch. How had it come to this? She had had so much faith in Coryn. She had been his first teacher in the Beyond. She had taught him how to dive for coals. Of course, he was such a natural that it only took him two blinks to learn. She had been there in the Beyond when he had taken that spectacular dive into Hrath'ghar and came back with the ember. Not even singed. But now he was being singed, so to speak, being weakened, damaged perhaps irreparably, by this strange blue owl.

CHAPTER NINETEEN
The Stink of a Hag

Bubo had stayed up the rest of the night working in his forge, juicing a coal. He peered out into the breaking dawn. He always thought that first light of twixt time was like a cold ember creeping over the horizon. Then the sun would heat up to a real sizzle, until it was full morning light. Bubo thought of everything in terms of coals and embers and flames. It was his measure, his tool, but when Otulissa had told him about the scraps of burnt paper and the book lift that she and Fritha had been flying, he was shocked. He had never thought of fire consuming parchment or paper before. Iron, metals — those were what one used fire for: to shape it, to make something new, to create something that didn't exist before. But burning paper? This made no sense whatsoever. It only destroyed. Metals — silver, iron, gold, these noble materials — were equal to the strikes of the hammer, perched on the throne of an anvil, ready to receive blows. But paper and parchment were noble in a different way.

Blank, clean, ready to receive the strokes of a quill dipped in ink or a brush tipped with paint. This burning of books was wrong. He had been so absorbed with these thoughts that he had not heard the approaching scratch of talons outside his cave.

"Bubo!"

The blacksmith wheeled around. *Coryn, already!* "Coryn, what brings you here?" Pelli had been right. He had not juiced that coal a moment too soon!

"Bubo, the time has come for me to have the ember again. I am the king. It belongs with me." He was speaking rapidly, giving too many reasons. Bubo knew that it would not be wise to give in too easily. It would only arouse suspicion. He must show some resistance.

"Have you discussed this with the Band?"

"The Band isn't here. You know that," Coryn said somewhat tersely.

"Well ... er ... yes ... but don't you think maybe you should wait until they return and discuss it with them then?"

"No, I don't see any advantage in waiting." He shook his head and his eyes seemed a dull, lusterless black. If Bubo hadn't known better, he'd think this owl was moon blinked.

"Well, I don't know, Coryn."

"I am your king. It is not for you to know."

These words, spoken in a dull, cold voice, stunned Bubo more than anything. Bubo sighed. "All right. Whatever you say." There was no response from Coryn. Bubo fetched the teardrop-shaped case and then his tongs. He poked down into the coal pit and pretended to search for several seconds and then plucked up the juiced ember. He dared not look at Coryn, but he sent a little prayer up to Glaux. Bubo was not really a praying kind of owl. So it was difficult for him to shape a prayer without some of his usual rough language. His prayers were more like strikes at the anvil then words of great reverence. *Racdrops! Let me pull this off, Glaux,* he thought. *Be a frinkin' shame were he to see this sprink ember for what it really is.* He slipped it into the teardrop-shaped case before Coryn could get a close look at it. It was just the green rim that worried him.

"There you be!" he said, handing the case to Coryn.

Coryn reached for it but did not meet Bubo's eyes. "Don't worry, Bubo. I'm different now." It was all Bubo could do not to say "Don't I know it." But he held his beak. Coryn was almost out of the cave when Bubo said, "Coryn." His voice was sharper. Coryn finally looked at him. Bubo skewered him with the intense gold of his eyes. "You do right by that ember, Coryn. You do right by her." Coryn suddenly looked stricken. He stumbled a bit. "Don't worry." His voice quaked. Then he repeated the words but this time there was a testy edge to his voice. "Don't worry."

"I am sorry, so sorry that these troubles have to be the reason for our first meeting. I have heard so much about you, Bess." Pelli was perched on the edge of a dictionary stand in the Palace of Mists. "And this place," she added, swiveling her head around. The stand held the largest dictionary she had ever seen. There were at least a thousand pages, with what must have been millions of words.

"Don't apologize, please. This situation sounds dire. And you were right to bring the ember here. Don't worry, I know a good place to hide it. But forgive me if I don't tell you where. It would only make it more dangerous for you."

"Yes, of course. The fewer who know about it the better." Pelli nodded in agreement. "But you have heard nothing of this blue owl's activities here on the mainland?"

"No, only at the great tree when Otulissa came with that young Pygmy . . ."

"Fritha?"

"Yes, Fritha, when they brought the books. I suppose." Bess nervously tapped the cabinet on which she perched with her foot. She began again. "I suppose I should have gone out and explored a bit. But I have a hard time leaving this place. It's . . . my . . . my weakness."

"Yes," Pelli replied softly. Soren had told her about this fear Bess had of leaving the Palace of Mists. "I don't think it's weakness, Bess. It's loyalty and love that keeps you here."

Bess just shook her head slowly. "I am not sure myself anymore. But whatever I can do here to help you, the Band, and the Guardians, I will. Rest assured."

"The Band did not stop here, did they?"

"No, I haven't seen a feather of them since they began the weather experiments Otulissa wrote me about."

"I wish I could find them. They sent a letter back to Coryn saying that they needed to extend their stay indefinitely."

"To Coryn? Didn't Soren write you a note?" Bess asked. Pelli shook her head. "How odd."

"Yes, I thought so, too." Pelli sighed. "Well, I must go straight back, before I am missed. I left the B's in Mrs. Plithiver's charge."

"Ah, Mrs. Plithiver. What an extraordinary creature."

"Indeed!"

Pelli had planned to go straight back. She would have had she not caught a glimpse of something flapping against the broad and mottled trunk of a sycamore tree. Going into a steep dive, she pulled out of it mid-trunk-level and hovered so she could read the piece of paper. It was a notice, written by a scribe undoubtedly, and tied to the tree with vines. She read it aloud to herself.

"*The four members of the Guardians of the Great Ga'Hoole Tree, known collectively throughout the owl kingdoms as the Band, were seen consorting with scrooms and dabbling in faithless acts of hagscraft. They were doing this under the cover of a so-called scientific expedition. Further information suggests that they have renounced their Guardian oath and switched their allegiance to the Northern Kingdoms. For this reason, the parliament of the Great Ga'Hoole Tree forbids anyone to welcome them into their hollows, speak to them, or transact any manner of business with them. Warning: These owls are considered dangerous.*'"

"I can't believe it!" Pelli said. A terrible bilious feeling rose in her gizzard. She thought she might be sick. She settled on a branch just below the notices, then flipped her head almost upside down and read it again. It was as if her entire world fell apart in that minute. Of course, not for one second did she believe it. "Get a grip!" she muttered and, in fact, tightened her grip on the slender branch where she perched. *Think, think, Pelli!* she counseled herself. She took several deep breaths. Her mind began to organize itself. Quietly, the thoughts came to her in a more orderly fashion. If the Band had seen this notice, their first instincts, she realized, would be to fly back to the great tree and say this was nothing but a pack of lies. "But that would be the last thing they *should* do," she whispered to herself. *Because,* she finished the thought in her head, *it must be some sort of trap!* And this is what she must tell them. But how to find them? How? *Mist!* Her gizzard and her brain suddenly twinkled with the thought. A light seemed to flood through her. They often visited Mist, or Hortense, as Soren and Gylfie called her. Hortense was the Glauxparent to the three B's. It was a long trip to Ambala but she would spend an even longer time searching for the Band. Mist and her two eagles and the snakes always seemed to know almost everything that was transpiring on the mainland. In the end, it would save her time if she went directly there. She would make up some excuse if she was really late coming back.

But a dread began to rise within her. Although the Striga didn't know she had left, if she were gone long enough to be missed, he would know that she might have seen the notices and then what? Well, she could not worry about that now. The most important thing was to alert the Band. Thank Glaux, she had gotten the Ember of Hoole out of there. "Thank Glaux," she murmured to herself. She only hoped that Bubo's ruse with the counterfeit ember had worked. It then dawned on her that the ember was not the only thing that was counterfeit. That letter Coryn had read! The one extending the Band's "experiments." Of course it was a fake! Hadn't she really known it all along? And besides that, there was nothing wrong with consorting with scrooms. Many owls had at one time or another in their lives encountered the scroom of a relative or dear friend. It was consorting with hagsfiends that was bad. And, in that moment, Pelli reached the same conclusion that her mate had: *This is hagscraft.*

She then had one further thought: *There's a hagsfiend in the great tree. It might be blue, it might look like an owl, fly like an owl. But it's haggish, I swear by Glaux!*

CHAPTER TWENTY

A Few Good Owls

Hortense had settled herself into one of the heart-wood branches high above the mossy dell of the Brad and watched quietly for a while. She reflected on all that she had learned in the last few days. When the Band had returned with the shocking news of the notice that had been posted of their exile and the horror of the charred remains of a burnt owl, Hortense asked them to repeat it, not once or twice, but three times. It was simply unbelievable. But there had been many things during her long life that at first had seemed unbelievable to her and that later she had come to realize were true. Almost as soon as she had sent the Band off to the Brad, Pelli had arrived with the news that things had deteriorated even further at the great tree, and that she and Otulissa and Bubo feared for the ember. And very shortly after all that, Slynella and Stingyll reported that a blue owl — known as Tengshu — had somehow found his way to the Brad. This, at least, was good news. The Band had told her of

124

this sage owl and now with his help a plan was taking shape for regaining the tree. If anyone could help the Band and the Guardians rid themselves of the Striga it would be this Tengshu from the Middle Kingdom. Although a sage, he was also a master of the fighting art of Danyar. And that was exactly what Tengshu was teaching the Ambala owls of the Brad now as Hortense looked down from her branch high in the heartwood grove. If the Band was to return to the great tree, they had to be prepared and they would need all the help they could get. As if this news was not enough, Gwyndor had also come to Hortense with rumors of something being planned for Balefire Night. Something bad.

Balefire Night occurred in the very last days of the season of the Copper Rose. It was one of the major holidays of the owl calendar and celebrated owlkind's command of fire, which began during the time of the legends; Grank was the first collier, and Theo was the first blacksmith. On this night, owls came together and built large bonfires making the night as bright as the day. There were contests of all sorts. Colliering contests, smithing competitions, flight games during which owls would compete to ride the intense thermal updrafts to new record heights. It was a joyous and boisterous holiday. Now with these rumors, who knew what Coryn, clearly under the influence of the Striga, was planning? But the Band must not rush back. It was truly a blessing that Tengshu had flown the River of Wind across the Sea of Vastness and found them. Hortense watched now as the one the Band called "the sage" instructed the owls in this strange method of warfare called Danyar. She had never seen anything like it. No battle claws, no fire branches, none of the traditional weapons; it was all about breathing. Breath was their major weapon. The Breath of Qui, as they called it, expanded the lungs of an owl and, when released, charged the owl's movement with great power. She was amazed at the progress made by these studious owls who had so recently devoted their lives to books. Their powers of concentration were great and undoubtedly this had helped them learn Danyar very quickly. There was a young Barred Owl, Austen, who was smashing the moss target to bits every time she hit it.

"Good, good. Excellent form, Austen!" Tengshu, with the slight Jouzhen lilt to his speech, exclaimed. "Watch Austen. Her preparation is excellent. Note how she lifts her wings ever so slightly at the beginning of the inhale."

A few minutes later, during a break in the training, Hortense flew down to the training level and hovered quietly until someone noticed her.

"Hortense!" Soren said, and swooped toward her. Immediately, he sensed something wrong. "What is it? Something about the three B's, Pelli?"

"Nothing worse, really, than what we already know." She sighed. The beads of moisture shimmered greenly in the dim light of the dell. "Pelli saw the signs of your 'faithless acts.'"

"What was she doing on the mainland?" Soren asked. "W-w-what could have brought her here now?"

"I'm getting to that," Hortense said patiently. An absolute hush had fallen on the Band and the other few owls who had gathered nearby. "She was on a mission to deliver the ember to an undisclosed location," she said gingerly. The Band immediately knew where it must be.

"So Coryn asked for it," Gylfie said somberly.

"Yes, and another was substituted," Mist replied.

"Bubo juiced one, didn't he?" Twilight said. "And that fool owl Coryn can't even tell the difference."

Soren wilfed as these words were spoken about his only nephew. But it was true. How had Coryn become such a fool? How had all this happened?

"And are there still rumors about Balefire Night?" Gylfie asked.

"Yes. They say it's going to be the biggest celebration ever."

"Yes, so much to burn," Soren said bitterly. None of the Band even dared think about the horrible charred skeleton they had found in that smoldering fire near where the notice had been posted. Suddenly, Soren thought of something. "If Pelli returns to the tree and tells the other owls, the parliament, about these things, surely . . ."

Hortense cut him off. "We discussed this, Soren. She is going to tell only a few owls. Otulissa, Bubo, Eglantine. She has to play it very cool right now. The Blue Brigade has infiltrated the tree. The Guardians are not out-numbered — yet. When was the last time there was a battle on the Island of Hoole?"

"The Siege," the four owls quickly replied.

"Exactly. It was bad. Strix Struma died and there were not nearly as many young'uns in the tree back then. This information of the Band being exiled is enough to trig-ger an uprising by the tree guardians. But they would lose — or suffer unthinkable losses. There can be no con-frontation until their numbers are strengthened. You have to return, ready with these new owls of the Brad properly trained." Hortense paused. She looked at the Band. "You have to remember, the four of you are sea-soned warriors. You have spent almost a lifetime in training. But here in Ambala we have seen little war. We have always lived, as I have said, on the edge of things."

"Madam," Tengshu interrupted, "I want to assure you these owls will be ready."

CHAPTER TWENTY-ONE
The Enemy Within

You see, Coryn. You have grown so much stronger. Now tell me truthfully, do you not feel better than ever in the presence of this ember?"

"Yes, it is true," Coryn agreed.

"You have strengthened your gizzard," the Striga said.

Coryn thought the Striga might be right. He no longer felt the deep twinges in his gizzard that he had when in the presence of the ember. But even before he had brought the ember from Bubo's forge, his gizzard had seemed to quiet in a way that gave him a new ease. Since he had been following the Striga's regime of spiritual cleansing by ridding himself of the vanities that had cluttered not so much his hollow, for those had been few, but his mind, life seemed easier. He no longer had the haunting visions of his mother, Nyra, and he finally began to realize that although he had loved his uncle Soren, this love had been a feckless indulgence on his part. It wasn't reciprocated in the way he had expected. He was basically excluded from the Band. He had never really understood this until the Striga pointed it out to him. He might be accepted as king by the great tree but never as a member of the Band by Soren and the others. And now there were two letters that confirmed this exclusion as truth. The first letter had arrived shortly before Punkie Night with its ridiculous talk about the necessity of extending the weather experiments. This second letter had just arrived, in which the Band reported that they had felt that they were not needed at the tree, and how had they put it? "Striga," Coryn said, "could you read that part of the letter to me again?"

"Certainly. 'As we do not feel that our presence at the tree is needed and that there are owls in the Northern Kingdoms who could benefit from our knowledge as rybs, we have decided to fly there for a short visit.'"

Coryn looked at the blue owl. "It is just as you predicted, isn't it? They are trying to make an alliance in the Northern Kingdoms without the consent of parliament."

"Negotiating independently. Why would any owl do such a thing? Treasonous, isn't it?" The Striga paused. "And treason is simply another face of vanity."

Coryn blinked. He supposed the Striga was right. Half a dozen moon cycles ago he might have questioned this logic. But somehow Coryn felt that he no longer had to question such notions or statements. There was a beautiful simplicity to everything that the Striga said. It would be difficult, however, to tell Pelli that her mate would be gone even longer. Pelli was a sweet, dear owl. He turned now to the Striga. "It's going to be hard to tell Pelli that Soren has extended his trip even longer and into the Northern Kingdoms."

"Yes, it will be. But you know, owls get over things. She has her children to keep her occupied. And let's be honest. Soren's first loyalty has never been to Pelli, but rather to the Band. At times, she must feel as excluded as you have felt."

"You know, you're right!" Coryn paused. "But I hesitate to tell her about this . . . this possible treason. I hope she doesn't suspect anything."

The Striga churred and shook his head. "I wouldn't worry, Coryn. Pelli is not all that bright, you know."

Coryn thought he felt a dim twinge in his gizzard, a split second of uncertainty about this last statement, but he chose to ignore it.

"I never knew about this place!" Bubo said with wonder. He glanced around at the thick, knotted roots. A scrim of threadlike taproots hung down, grazing their heads.

"When I came to the tree to live here and be Soren's mate, he and the Band and Otulissa took me here," Pelli said.

"We didn't want to keep any secrets from Pelli," Otulissa added. "They were mates. There should never be secrets between mates. There are a few others who know about it. The Chaw of Chaws. But it was brilliant of Pelli to think of having the parliament meeting here. There are too many strangers about to speak freely in the parliament hollow. I mean, since when have we allowed outsiders into the parliament meetings? These owls that have been hanging around since Punkie Night, what gives them the right?" Otulissa huffed indignantly.

"So, let me get this straight," Bubo said. "You can hear the parliament when you're down here in the roots, but they can't hear you?"

"Yes, it's strictly a one-way system," Otulissa said.

"It's really the most secure place in the tree. There's no other place we could all meet except here. And no one will miss us at this hour," Pelli said.

"I just hope we can all cram in here." Bubo looked around.

Otulissa glanced about, then blinked. There was a slightly mournful tinge in her amber eyes.

The word had been passed to the other members of the parliament. They would be led to the roots by Martin, Eglantine, and Ruby — other members of the Chaw of Chaws. Immediately upon Pelli's return, she told Otulissa and Bubo about the notice accusing the Band of treason, and they decided that something must be done. But they did not want to act rashly. Their first step was taking a wing count of the additional owls who were roosting in the outer branches of the tree and the guest hollows, which had been filled since Punkie Night. Guests often came to the tree but never had so many lingered for so long. And now with the latest news of the letter that Coryn had just received — which she felt was as counterfeit as the ember Bubo had juiced — they were convinced that they were in the most dire circumstances. They all dreaded the approaching Balefire Night. They must be prepared. But to fight a battle on their own island in their own tree was simply too risky. The hardest thing Pelli had ever had to do was to feign stupidity when Coryn had summoned her and read the second letter. First of all, she had to pretend that she believed every word of the forged document. She had to appear simple and trusting. But all the while, her mind was ticking and her gizzard sizzling. Simulating ignorance was her best defense. She had begun to plan before Coryn had even finished reading the letter and she would not let her first instincts or impulses get the better of her.

Two by two, the owls of the parliament crept down into the hidden chamber deep within the roots of the great tree.

"Even though this particular place in the tree is virtually soundproof, I suggest that we keep our voices low." Pelli looked around at the members of the parliament. Some of them, like Elvanryb, were very old and had been members of the parliament for years. Some, like Sylvana, a beautiful Burrowing Owl and masterful ryb of the tracking chaw, were relatively new to the parliament. But they were all now in this small space, their eyes glistening with a mixture of apprehension and perhaps a glint of hope. They had felt depressed by the state of their king, concerned by the new owls hanging around the tree, and utterly contemptuous of the one called the Striga.

"We are safe here," Pelli said. She felt it was important for them to be at ease. "What I am about to show you is shocking. But not for a moment do I believe it. And neither should you." Pelli unfurled the notice she had found on the tree. The owls gathered close and read it, their beaks dropping open one by one as they took in the heinous accusations.

"Outrageous!" Elvanryb said in a hot whisper. "I don't believe it for one second."

"Nor do I." Several of the other owls of the parliament shook their heads vigorously.

"How did you get this?" Sylvana asked.

"I flew to the mainland with the real Ember of Hoole."

There was utter silence.

"You mean that's not the real ember in Coryn's hollow?" said Poot, a Boreal Owl who had flown with the weather chaw for years.

"No, it's a fake. I juiced it," Bubo said.

"Then what's his excuse? Why is Coryn acting yoicks?"

Pelli shook her head. "I'm not sure. I know that Coryn suffered things when he was young with Nyra, horrible things that none of us could ever imagine. But now is not the time to think about that. We have to act. When I read this malicious notice, my first thought was: If the Band has seen this, they will fly directly back to the great tree, but then I realized . . ."

"It's a trap," Elvanryb said quietly.

"Exactly, Elvanryb, a trap. Look at all the new owls in the tree who have come since Punkie Night. Something's up."

____ ____ ___ what can we do?" Poot asked.

____ _____ued, "We must keep up a show of igno-

___ it is my good luck to be considered almost witless by the Striga. And Coryn seems to agree with everything the Striga says. But we must be prepared when the time comes."

"What should we do?" Martin asked.

"I think Otulissa can speak to this."

Otulissa stepped forward. She cocked her head and looked directly at Sylvana. "Sylvana, you were crucial to our success during the siege. I think we must call upon you again. We need to move the ice weapons from their cold storage burrow. I don't want these new owls knowing anything about them. Any ideas, Sylvana?"

"Yes," she replied. "There is an old tunnel in the roots, on the other side of the tree from where we are now. I'll get it cleaned out."

"Does Coryn know about the ice weapons?" Poot asked.

"He might know about them," Sylvana said. "But since he has been at the tree we have never fought with them. The last time was in the Battle of the Burning."

"Precisely," Martin said. "And that could be a problem. Ruby, Otulissa, and I are the only owls here right now who have ever fought with the ice weapons. We were on that first expedition to the Northern Kingdoms where we trained with old Moss and the Glauxspeed and the Frost Beaks units. We're out of practice."

"Get in practice." It was Quentin, a grizzled old Barred Owl who, as long as anyone could remember had been the quartermaster of the great tree, in charge of weapons and military equipment. "I've been tending those ice weapons like they were new hatchlings all these years, just exactly according to Ezylryb's instructions. They are in perfect condition. The ice picks sharp as talons. The ice scimitars got as keen an edge as anything Bubo could forge. What they need are owls who can wield them."

"But when can we practice? Where?" Martin asked.

Pelli looked at Sylvana. "Sylvana, is that tunnel big enough for owls to hone their ice weapons skills in secret?"

"I suppose so. But how do we train enough owls without being noticed — even in secret?"

Martin, who was particularly gifted with the ice splinter, having trained directly under Colonel Frost Blossom of the Frost Beak division, stepped forward. The little Northern Saw-whet looked at the owls. "When it comes down to it, we'll be fighting in tight quarters, around, perhaps, or even in the tree. We don't need a

...ll we need is a few good owls.

_ owls crammed into the small, confined chamber of roots looked at one another. *A few good owls!* The words stirred their gizzards and made their hearts beat stronger. They were those owls!

CHAPTER TWENTY-TWO
A Singed Blue Feather

Never for the rest of his life would Cory forget stepping outside the burrow he shared with his sister, Kalo, and her family in The Barrens that tween time and catching sight of the singed blue feather quivering in the light breeze. He wilfed and felt his gizzard turn to stone. "We're marked!" Then he silently cursed his sister, the owl he loved most in the entire world. *Her frinkin' books! Racdrops! Why has she clung to them so long? Why after the burning did she salvage the scraps of paper and try to piece them back together?* When he had confronted her with this and asked her how, as a mother, she could have done this, she had replied, "Simply because I am a mother. I owe it to my hatchlings to learn all that I can."

There was no arguing with Kalo. Her husband, Grom, was a quiet, reflective owl, who rarely contradicted his mate. Marked by the blue feather! This was the limit, in Cory's mind. Now she had done it. They would all have to go into hiding. A singed blue feather was the death warrant. Once a hollow, nest, or burrow had been marked with it, an owl would stand trial — trial by fire — for keeping an unclean habitat, a home profaned by the "vanities" and "skart" literature that they had refused to yield up. It was an odd test. If the owl could escape the strong fibrous green vines that bound them to the stake, and fly away while reciting the Glaux creed rejecting all vanities, then that owl was declared innocent of all charges. But so far no owl had escaped.

Cory knew of two burnings and suspected more. The creed itself was controversial. No one had ever heard of it before the Blue Brigade had appeared. It was a jumble of words about the hagsfires, lustrous pearls, rich fabrics, and the dark and haggish ink of skart pages printed by the "monster": the printing press. More and more charred piles of these so-called vanities littered the landscape on the mainland. And with the Blue Brigade patrolling everywhere, owls stayed in their burrows and hollows whenever possible. Cory stumbled back and headed toward Kalo's burrow. He heard the soft crying before he got there.

"Grom!" he called out to Kalo's mate, hardly more than a heap of feathers collapsed in a corner of the burrow. The Burrowing Owl looked up. His face had feathered gray overnight. The white swag of feathers above his eyes had thickened, as had the one beneath his beak. "She's gone," he sobbed.

"Then she saw it? The blue feather?"

"I guess so. She left me this note." He handed Cory a scrap of paper.

My dear mate, my brother Coryn, and my little owlet,

You must understand, all of you, how deeply I regret endangering my own family. But in truth, every owl in every one of the five kingdoms is endangered, for we're not talking about losing our "vanities" here. We're talking about losing the right to think. Books can be burned. But the ideas and the knowledge in them cannot be killed. Owls can die, but books, never. Fear of ideas is the most extreme form of cowardice. I have love in my gizzard and heart; they only have hatred. I have inspiration from the books I have read; they only have terror from the lies they have chosen to believe. I have heroes, like Siv and King Hoole; Grank, the first collier; and Theo the peaceful blacksmith. They have no one but that twisted blue owl. So don't worry about me. These owls who hunt me are more cowardly and more defenseless than I am, for they have stopped thinking.

Glauxspeed,

Kalo

"I'm going to find her," Cory said.

"I knew you would say that." Grom looked up as if seeking an answer. "But what has happened to that friend of hers, that Barn Owl we thought was to be the noblest of kings? The one you were named after?"

It was then that an idea came to Cory. He turned around to leave the burrow.

"You're leaving?" Grom asked. "Going to find her, right now?"

"No, I am going to see a king, a king who was once noble."

As Cory angled north by northeast to catch the wind, he noticed that the border between Silverveil and his own scoured landscape, The Barrens, seemed different. The verdant lushness of one of the most beautiful forests in the Southern Kingdoms, like a cloth of green plush with trees and undulating meadows and valleys, usually rose up in sharp contrast to The Barrens. But now he noticed bare patches in the tree line along the border, and when he crossed over, the terrain below appeared scarred and scorched in places. He saw smoldering pyres and his gizzard writhed. *They are everywhere*, he thought. *Wherever will Kalo hide?* Yes, Balefire Night was coming, but these piles of wood and brush were much more numerous than those usually prepared for the celebration.

In a clearing below, he saw a gathering of owls. Something was about to be ignited. *Great Glaux! It's an owl — it's four owls.* He felt his gizzard turn to stone. *I am going yeep,* he thought. The ground was rushing toward him. His vision suddenly narrowed, tunnel-like, its edges a radiant blur as the ground rushed up. He felt the wind press through his feathers. His eyes dried out. A hiss filled his ear slits. It was the noise of his body gathering speed. *I am going to die,* he thought. But then he felt something grab his neck. Talons gripped him. He was floating up again. The ground receded. He could see the moon, the stars, and then the dark embroidery of pine needles.

"There's a hollow right up here, buddy."

Cory looked up. A Masked Owl was clutching him.

"Thought you bit it." The owl smelled like charred wood, coal, fire!

"You going to burn me?" Cory asked.

"Are you yoicks? There's enough burning around here. It's these blue-feather thugs. They steal coals from my forge to start their haggish fires."

Cory almost fainted with relief. The Masked Owl was a Rogue smith. There was a famous one in Silverveil he had heard of from Kalo. In fact, if he recalled correctly, this Rogue smith had been a good friend to the king, when the king was a young'un living with his terrible mother in the canyonlands.

"Well, that was certainly a close one," the Rogue smith said, tucking Cory into the hollow.

"What are they doing down there? Are they burning owls?"

"Not yet. Just dummies — effigies, I think they call them."

"Effigies of whom?" Cory asked.

"Well, I'm not sure. Let's have a peek. You feel steady enough?"

"Yes," Cory replied and followed the Rogue smith out to the end of a long limb.

Below them on the ground were four figures made from bundles of twigs and dried grasses. One was very large and was covered with a silvery lichen called old bird's beard. Another was made of reddish twigs with a face that was almost white and two black coals for eyes. The third was a bundle of twigs with two long sticklike legs, and the fourth was a little ball of frizzled tumbleweed. Four owls, each a different species: a Great Gray, a Barn Owl, a Burrowing Owl, and an Elf Owl. Gwyndor, the Rogue smith of Silverveil, for it was he, swiveled his head and looked at Cory. "The Band," he said quietly. "They are burning the Band in effigy." And just then a dozen or so owls, each sporting a blue feather, swooped around the effigies. A grim chant rose from them.

Fire does redemption bring
Cleansing flames for which we sing.
Scour the soul, prepare the mind,
Make us to all vanities blind.
Bring your gaudies, profane art,
Singe it, burn it, all is skart!
Let there be nought but ash,
Make redemption ours at last.

As they sang, owls came forward, dropping strands of beads, books, whirligigs, and all sorts of articles onto the pyre. A large Horned Owl flew up to the pyre with a torch and touched it to the kindling. There were cracks and popping sounds as pearls and glass exploded. As the flames licked higher and closer to the effigies of the Band, the figures began to jiggle in a weird palsied dance as if trying to escape. And then the red tongues reached them and they were devoured in one fiery gulp. A cheer went up, but Cory noticed that the cheers came only from the Blue Brigade. The other owls remained silent and wilfed as the fire grew hotter and hotter. The scent of sizzling glue rose from the books and with it the sad odor of the incinerating lovely things.

* * *

In the dell of Ambala a new kind of training had begun. This training involved learning to fly dressed in draperies of moss.

"How am I suppose to do my famous flying wedgie with all this stuff hanging off me?" Twilight grumbled.

"Put a mouse in it, Twilight, and pay attention." Gylfie scowled.

"That's easy for you to say. You're so itty-bitty one little patch of moss covers you up."

"It's all relative," Digger said. His legs were cloaked in a very green moss called bunch clover. The owls of Ambala had introduced them to one of their oldest traditions for Balefire Night celebrations: Greenowling. The tradition could be traced back to an ancient poem of Ambalan origin:

> *In a night sky drenched in flames*
> *Thus begin the Balefire games.*
> *Then high above the conflagration*
> *Comes the brightest green formation.*
> *Robed in Ambala's greenest green*
> *Their brains so fit, their gizzards keen,*
> *"Greenowls" is their special name.*
> *Cloaked in moss they play the game*
> *Merry, fast, and fair they play*

Until the night fades into day.
The fires die, begin to smolder,
The embers grow cold, then colder.
Another Balefire come and gone
Ambala's Greenowls praised in song.

On Balefire Night, with battle claws tucked into their mossy garments and branches ready to ignite, the Band would end their exile and reclaim the great tree. If the king must die . . . well, they tried not to think of that. But if it did come to that, they must be prepared. Soren had been ready to kill his own brother, Kludd, and was only spared from delivering those fatal blows because Twilight had hurled himself into the fray, impaling Kludd on a firebrand. But would Soren kill the son of Kludd — his own nephew — if need be?

He would do anything to protect Pelli, the three B's, and the great tree. He was, after all, a mate, a father, and finally, a Guardian of Ga'Hoole.

CHAPTER TWENTY-THREE
Something Familiar?

Y ou mean I can't see the king?" Cory asked.

"Why should you be able to see him? You're just an ordinary owl," a Barred Owl replied. The owl sported a blue feather tucked into the coverts of his primary feathers.

"I have very important business." Cory didn't want to say his real name. He remembered how the awful blue owl had ordered that Kalo be dragged from the burrow, and then sneered at her when she had said his name. He had claimed that to name an owl "Coryn" was blasphemous. It was Cory's third night at the tree and still he had not seen the king for whom he had been named. Suddenly, that same hideous blue owl stuck his head out of the port of the king's hollow.

"What does this Burrowing Owl want?" he asked.

"To see the king. Claims he has business of a personal nature. He's getting tiresome."

Suddenly, Cory got an idea. He would change tactics. Anything to get in. "It's not really of a personal nature," he blurted out. "I mean, this person used to be my friend, but I want to report a suspected hoarding incident." The Blue Brigade owls were always keen to hear of hoarding incidents. "Let him in," said the Striga.

Great! Cory thought. Now if he could just see the king alone! But they were not alone. The Striga perched nearby. What could he say to the king with that horrid owl right there? And the king seemed odd, not at all kingly. His feathers were dull and lusterless. He had heard gossip that the king rarely left his hollow. He was standing in front of a small case that glowed with the light of an ember and was staring at it. *Could this be the Ember of Hoole that I have heard so much about?* Cory wondered.

"What is it?" the king asked without turning around to look at the owl.

"A hoarding incident to report," the Striga said.

The king sighed. It was a sigh of boredom more than anything else. He continued peering at the ember. He felt none of the old exhilarating tingle he used to feel when around the ember. The Striga was right. He had grown stronger in its presence. "It's chilly in here," he finally said. "Could you poke up the fire in the grate, Striga?"

"Yes, it's beginning to flurry outside," Cory said.

The king turned around slowly. Was there something familiar in the timbre of that voice? He looked at the young owl and blinked. *Who is this owl?*

And while that disturbing thought swirled in the king's mind, Cory wished that he could be alone with him for only a minute or two.

"A hoarding incident," the Striga prompted.

"Yes. I think this owl has been wrongly accused. And I know that King Coryn . . ."

Something twitched in Coryn's gizzard. There was something about the way this young owl said Coryn's name that seemed like a distant echo of something long ago. The fires in the grate burst into a lively blaze. Cory stood between the king and the grate. The young king suddenly pushed him aside. The gesture was misinterpreted by both the Striga and Cory.

"He wants you out! Now!" the Striga commanded.

"But I haven't said what I have to say," Cory pleaded.

Before Cory knew it, two guards hustled him from the hollow and the king had done nothing to stop them. But Coryn had spied something in the flames. Something alarming. Something terrifying. "Leave me alone," Coryn said when the Striga returned. The blue owl silently retreated. Coryn continued to stare into the fire. How had he let himself forget his gift? Coryn could see things in flames. But how long had it been since he had even looked into a fire? It was a skill that the Striga knew nothing about.

And I must not let him know! Coryn thought. For the first time in many moon cycles Coryn felt a true tremor in his gizzard. It was as if it had been dead, insentient as a rock, but now it was awakening.

He was seeing shapes in the flames. The first shape was that of an ember, and in its center a lick of blue and then there was the shimmering edge of green. *How could I have forgotten that green?* His eyes widened. He spun about and gazed at the ember in the case.

"It's a fake," he whispered to himself. "How could I have not known?" And the young owl who had just been in the hollow, the Burrowing Owl? He had never even asked his name but he knew it was Coryn, brother of Kalo — Coryn hatched from the egg he had rescued long ago. *Great Glaux, what has happened to me?* He looked again at the counterfeit ember. *I cannot blame the ember this time. Yes, I have been weak. The Striga has groomed and nurtured a great weakness in me, through flattery. The very methods used to render the owls of the Dragon Court weak and powerless! Stupid! How stupid of me!* But he was done with being stupid. He flew out of his hollow and was about to command that the Striga come to see him immediately. But he stopped short. Who were all these new owls and why were they all wearing blue feathers? He had thought that the Blue Feather Club was just a silly owlet thing. Something for the young'uns. He felt a bilious surge in his gizzard. Where were his trusted Guardians? The true Guardians of Ga'Hoole? The Band was away — he knew that. But what about Pelli, Eglantine, Otulissa, for Glaux's sake? He realized he had hardly seen them except in the dining hollow. Something definitely was up.

The Striga flew down onto the branch where Coryn perched. "Sir, a problem?" The blue owl had sensed something. Coryn felt his gizzard clench painfully. But it was a welcome pain. He was feeling again, thinking again. He was regaining his wits and in that moment he knew that he must appear as witless as ever. "No, nothing wrong. Now tell me, what are the plans for Balefire Night?"

"Well, yes. We are going to build a very large bonfire — the largest ever — and it will be the final stage of the special relinquishment ceremonies." Coryn felt a chill run through his gizzard. He knew about "special" ceremonies. His mother, Nyra, had invented several; one in particular required that Coryn murder a friend.

But now he couldn't escape, nor did he want to. He was the king of this great tree. The tree was still great but his own honor was gone. He had let this happen and now he must take responsibility for restoring his honor and order to the tree. He returned to his hollow and peered into the flames again. Was that a reflection in the golden light? Was it his own flickering image? He took a step closer to the grate. "Who is it?" he whispered to the flames. He heard a slithering on the edge of his hollow. Mrs. Plithiver slid into the hollow, carrying a nut cup of milkberry tea.

"Mrs. P., what are you doing here?"

"I was on my way to visit with Audrey, and I thought I perceived a new stirring in a gizzard that — How should I put it? Has not stirred for a while."

Coryn blinked. "Yes, Mrs. P." Coryn nodded slowly and lowered his voice. "A gizzard has stirred."

"My coronation teacup . . . I don't know where it is," Madame Plonk had said to the Barred Owl who had flown into her hollow without even asking. And it was true, Madame Plonk did not know where it was. The Barred Owl believed her and left. Octavia, her nest-maid snake, pretended to snooze in a fat coil in the corner of the hollow. It was certainly not the hollow it had once been. Stripped of all ornamentation, the spinning glass whirligigs, the plush velvet cushions, the embroidered cloth, the niches that spilled with beads. Most of them had been seized but Doc Finebeak had managed to sneak a few off the island, and Octavia herself had tucked the teacup away very soon after the first relinquishing ceremonies had begun some nights ago. Although Doc Finebeak had planned to leave right after Punkie Night, Madame Plonk had begged to stay through Balefire Night as she was sure singing would be permitted.

Since Punkie Night, things had deteriorated. Too many strangers had stayed on at the tree after the celebration. The great grass harp had mysteriously suffered new damage. So there had been no song night after night. And now as he entered the hollow he shared with his dear Plonkie, he found her in tears. Between sobs she explained what had happened.

"Don't worry, my dear. It is safe," he whispered. But he was agitated and again frustrated that he had not insisted upon their leaving earlier. Just then, Octavia lifted her head. "Oh, Octavia," Madame Plonk gasped, "you won't believe what happened."

"Yes, I will. No — don't waste your breath explaining, dearie." She swung her head toward Doc Finebeak. "Doc, you need to go to Bubo's forge. Otulissa is waiting there for you. I think she might have something . . ." She hesitated. "Something *hopeful* to tell you."

The fires of the forge were crackling noisily. And Bubo was beating the daylights out of a chunk of redmore, a particularly hard kind of rock that yielded a high grade of metal. He saw Doc coming and nodded him into the cave. Doc quickly realized that Bubo meant the whanging and banging of his hammer on the anvil and the cracklings of the hot fires in the forge to serve as a bulwark of noise so that Otulissa could speak to him without fear of being overheard. Quickly, she divulged the secret training that was going on in the old tunnel. She explained how Bubo had juiced the counterfeit ember. Doc's gizzard sang when he heard this news. They needed his help. She had explained that there were few of them in on the plan as they did not want to arouse suspicion. She also told him how Pelli, after her trip to hide the real ember, had gone to see Hortense and told her of the happenings. From Hortense, she found out that the Band was aware of the dire conditions at the tree. They would be coming back soon with help. But Otulissa and Pelli and Bubo felt that more was needed now.

"Doc, can you help us?" she whispered desperately. "We know that in your tracking days you met all sorts of owls, including hireclaws."

Almost before Otulissa had finished speaking, he was heading to fetch the black feather that allowed him to fly freely any time of the day, safe from mobbings by crows. It was mid-morning. Most of the tree was asleep and it was the perfect time for him to leave. He did not even say good-bye to Plonkie. Better that she not know.

CHAPTER TWENTY-FOUR
Once Upon a Time

He knows?" Pelli gaped at Mrs. P. "Coryn knows, and he isn't angry, Mrs. P.?"

"Only at himself, my dear. You see, his gizzard is awakening, stirring."

"He can't let the Striga know."

"Of course not. He must play dumb, as you have done. But he feels terrible and he is ready to help in any way he can."

"Did you tell him about what we are doing?"

"Not yet. I only said that I would consult with you and Otulissa."

"How do you account for it, Mrs. P., his awakening, as you call it?"

"Well." She sighed. "It could be one of several things. When I went in the hollow he was staring into the fire in the grate."

"Flame reading," Pelli said suddenly. "He probably hasn't done it for a long time."

"Yes, but I don't think it was just that. A young Burrowing Owl arrived several nights ago, begging to see Coryn. He finally got in to see him. I have felt that young owl's extreme agitation ever since he arrived. I saw him leave Coryn's hollow and it was precisely in that moment that I got my first inkling . . . glimmer of the stirrings in Coryn's gizzard."

"You are remarkable, Mrs. P.!" Pelli said.

"Well, you know, it comes with the scales." Her rose-colored scales seemed to shimmer as she said this.

While Mrs. Plithiver conversed with Pelli, Coryn stepped out of his hollow for the first time in a long while to explore the great tree. It was nearly a moon cycle since he had gone beyond the branch outside his hollow. Things had changed drastically. First of all, there were many new owls, owls he didn't recall seeing before. But there were other changes as well. He flew into the Great Hollow and up to the gallery of the grass harp. He tottered as he settled on a perch. "What in the world?" he muttered. The lovely curving frame of the harp was blank and its strings lay in a tangled pile. He remembered talk about damage to the harp and recalled that the Striga said they should not rush to repair it. And then it burst upon him. His gizzard was racked with fear, shame. Great Glaux! He realized that it had been many, many nights since he had last heard the voice of Madame Plonk. He rushed out of the Great Hollow to find her.

On his way, he saw more signs of the terrible changes that had occurred. Peeking into Mainz, the press hollow where the printers could usually be heard chatting softly, he found all was silent. The inkwells were caked with dried ink. The press itself was strung with cobwebs. He rushed on to the hollow of the lacemakers' guild. There was no sound of the caller chanting the instructions for the particular designs. Absent was the soft whirring of the bobbins, unfurling thread as the four pairs of lacing snakes wove the thread through a series of patterns. Their perches were empty.

He heard a stirring coming from a corner in the lacemakers' hollow. It was a very young nest-maid snake. "What happened here?" Coryn asked.

"Not much!" the nest-maid fumed. "I got here less than a moon cycle ago and was told that the lacemakers' guild had been disbanded. Everything's changed here. At least from the way it was." The snake sighed again. "Once upon a time . . ." Then the nest-maid seemed suddenly alert. "Hey, who are you?"

Coryn felt a flutter in his gizzard. This nest-maid was

new and probably never had met him before. But nest-maids were keen and this one seemed to realize he was someone special.

"Oh," Coryn quickly said, "I've been away, too, for quite a while. Yes, things seemed to have changed."

"It's not just the lacemakers' guild that has been dis-banded, but the weavers' and the printers' guilds, too. No pun intended, but even the Band seems to have been disbanded."

Coryn's gizzard clenched so painfully, he groaned.

"You all right?" the snake asked.

He coughed. "Yes, I'll be fine. You are right. Once upon a time, things were very different here in this great tree."

CHAPTER TWENTY-FIVE
Flames Within Flames

As he left the lacemakers' hollow, Coryn felt an urgent need to find that young Burrowing Owl who had tried to speak to him. *That owl had something vitally important to tell me. I need to find him. But how? Where?* Coryn went back to his hollow and looked deeply into the flames again. For too long he had ignored his gift of firesight.

"Sir! Sir! Your Majesty." Coryn heard an unfamiliar voice behind him. He turned and saw a Short-eared Owl enter his hollow.

"Yes?"

"Your Majesty, the Striga has suggested that I keep you company."

"As you wish," Coryn said, "but do not speak to me," and he turned his gaze back to the flames. The Short-eared Owl, who wore a blue feather tucked between his coverts, stood in the shadows, watching Coryn study the flames.

No two flames were ever exactly alike and yet they all possessed the same structures. It was the central yellow curved plane of the flame that yielded the images.

He blinked, then his eyes opened in wonder. There was a familiar shape, a space from his past. The cave in the canyonlands where he had experienced firesight for the first time! How ironic that this extraordinary gift had been revealed at the Marking ceremony in which his father's bones had been burned! Coryn felt his gizzard quicken, his mind suddenly keen. Within the cave, other shapes began to take form, but the one that riveted his attention was a dearly known one — his friend, his only friend from that long time ago, Phillip, the Sooty Owl, the very owl his mother had murdered. The flames curled in, engulfing the image. The yellow plane quivered and grew longer, more slender. Another owl shape revealed. Unmistakable in its length and elegance. Kalo! She was perched on an immense fallen trunk. He knew that tree trunk because he had lived there as an outcast when he had fled the Pure Ones, years before. He tipped closer to the fire in his grate. Felt the warmth on his beak. *These flames are telling me of my friends. Phillip is gone and . . . and . . .* He blinked and looked deeper into the very gizzard of the fire. Something was burning within the flames. There were flames within the flames, another fire, and at its center was Kalo! But suddenly the shape that was Kalo dissolved into ashes and another took its place. A smaller owl. It was the young Burrowing Owl who tried to speak with Coryn. "My namesake! Coryn!"

"Sir?" said the Short-eared Owl. "Your what?"

"Namesake." He said the word slowly. Coryn's eyes widened into a seemingly vacant stare as he looked at the Short-eared Owl. The images of the fire were replaying in his mind's eye, stirring the innermost part of his gizzard. He knew Kalo was in the Shadow Forest. She was safe, but not for long. Of this, he was sure. For now, the images yielded by the flames and the words of the Striga began to weave together into a diabolical design. *So this is to be the great and special relinquishment ceremony that is to mark Balefire Night.*

It all came to Coryn in a single piece. Owls would be burned in the flames of Balefire Night. Of course, only a few owls knew what was planned, only those closest to the Striga. They were now hunting down the offenders to the way of perfect simplicity. And Kalo was not a simple owl. She loved to think, to read. He remembered her well. It all made perfect sense now that her brother had come to seek his help — help from the king whose name he bore.

"Are you all right, sir? You look like you've seen a scroom."

"Perhaps I have," Coryn replied quietly. He moved away from the fire and flew onto the perch near the portal.

"Where are you going, sir?"

Coryn thought quickly. He was going to the Shadow Forest, but he did not want this blue-feathered owl to know. So he replied almost casually, "To the spirit woods, of course." He paused and blinked at the Short-eared Owl. "That is where scrooms can be found, you know."

Getting away was very easy for Coryn. The dawn was just breaking. The owls had been up past twixt time preparing the fires for Balefire Night, which would be set the coming night. They were so exhausted that most had not even gone to the dining hollow for breaklight but repaired immediately to their hollows for sleep. Coryn left his hollow and flew off into that dawn to save Kalo, sister of another owl named Coryn whom he had saved once before. This time he might save himself as well.

"He what?" said the Striga, blinking his eyes rapidly. "He's going to the spirit woods?"

"Yes, sir."

"I suppose one only goes to such a place to consort with scrooms." The Striga paused, and churred softly. "How convenient. Yes, how very convenient. A king — a so-called king consorting with scrooms. This is worse than any vanity. Why . . . why, it's hagscraft!" *And by the time he returns*, thought the Striga, *this great tree will be mine. These kingdoms, these five kingdoms will be mine and the true redemption shall begin. For I have flown through the shadows of faith, have been lured by the deadliest of vanities, have scoured and plucked myself so I am the perfect vessel for this kingship.*

The Striga was nearly overwhelmed by his own sense of perfection. The tree would be his soon. And if anyone had any doubts about his right to rule this great tree, he knew that there were now enough of his elite fighting unit, the Blue Brigade, to take the tree by force. But there might be very little need for force after the climactic moment of the Balefire Night festivities — the special relinquishing ceremonies. No one would dare oppose him after that.

CHAPTER TWENTY-SIX

The Last Design

It's the Greenowls of Ambala!" A hearty cheer rose up from the grog tree where owls were just beginning to celebrate Balefire Night. They churred and hooted as scores of owls draped in cloaks of greenest moss and lichen flew by overhead.

"Ain't seen them out for Balefire Night in a long time."

"Naw, they usually keep to themselves, those owls of Ambala," said another.

"Don't quite have the gizzard for Balefire this year meself," a Whiskered Screech muttered. "Not with all them owls sporting the blue feathers."

"Lousy bunch."

"Hush, they got spies all over." A Pygmy Owl fluttered down and put out a nut cup for a spot of bingle juice.

"They say the king's useless now. Gone yeep in his own hollow — never comes out."

Coryn's gizzard twisted painfully as he overheard this last remark. He had taken a detour on his way to the

Shadow Forest because it had suddenly struck him that he was unarmed. If he went to a Rogue smith he would be recognized, but he could perhaps sneak some coals from a Balefire. He knew from times past that this particular grog tree kept a Balefire, but most of the owls were too occupied with their drinking to keep a close watch on the fire, which was a short distance from the base of the grog tree's trunk. They might play a few games around it as the evening wore on but, for now, they were enjoying the bingle juice and the song of a rather off-key gadfeather. The owls gathered into a tighter clump in the lower branches as the gadfeather began a new verse. Now would be the perfect time to fetch the coals, along with the dis-carded botkin on a chain he had seen near the fire to carry them in. He kept a careful watch, and when all the owls had congregated on the other side of the tree far from the Balefire, he stole down and in one swift pass grabbed the botkin and chain and plucked some coals from the very heart of the fire to fill it.

He was off before the gadfeather had even finished the first bars of the song. He headed as fast as he could fly toward the Shadow Forest, the place he'd seen in the flames where he thought he might find Kalo or his name-sake, Cory.

*   *   *

He slowed his flight as he approached the tree, then felt his gizzard swim up when he heard the voices of two owls.

He flew into the thickest branches of a black spruce, blinked and focused on the two owls who were flying low around the fallen tree, sometimes lighting down and peering into a crack or hole.

"She ain't here! But she's been here not long ago."

"Yep. I see fresh pellets. Some molted feathers."

"Hope she's not going through an early molt. The Striga and Field Marshal Cram want all the owls that we're supposed to bring to the island in full feather. Burn better that way."

Coryn's gizzard throbbed with disgust and hatred.

"Scouring. That's the word we're supposed to use. Scouring — not burning — remember? That's the one the Striga always uses. It's their redemption. Cleanse them so they can rise to glaumora."

Coryn had stopped listening to this trash. He opened the botkin and broke off a branch from the tree and then broke that one in half again.

"Hey, what's that noise? Something in that tree!"

And at that very instance, Coryn flew out of the tree with two flaming branches.

"Time for a scouring!" he bellowed.

"It's the king!" The scar running down his face gleamed like an ice seam in the white feathers of his face. The two owls fumbled with their battle claws. They were big owls. One was a Great Gray, one a Great Horned. Coryn was much smaller. But he had two things on his side: surprise and fire weapons. He had learned firefighting from the Chaw of Chaws. The Great Gray extended his battle talons and was scooping under the flaming branches for a heart rip. But he was coming in too fast, which would wreck his aim and so, with a dodge and a swat, Coryn threw him off. Still, he was a bold fighter, this Great Gray. *A match for Twilight,* Coryn thought. How he wished Twilight were here. Coryn was sweeping the branches in wide arcs to set up a defensive ring of sparks around him that he hoped would keep the owls at bay. But he could not keep fighting defensively. It would tire him out. He had to hurt these owls or kill them.

Suddenly, there was a blur at the edge in the narrow cone of his vision. To see more he would have to turn his head, but he must keep his eyes focused on the two owls who were trying to break through the ring of sparks. What was it on the edge of his vision? Whatever it was quickly caught the owls' attention. They turned and in that second he felt his flaming branch shake.

"Kalo!" She had rushed up with a branch of her own and ignited it from his. But Kalo was not the only thing on the edge of his sight. He spied a rabbit hopping about below. It was popping in and out of the hollow trunk of the fallen tree, distracting the Great Horned and the Great Gray. Coryn blinked in disbelief. It was his friend the rabbit, the mystic rabbit who read webs. The creature had distracted the two owls just long enough for Kalo to sweep in and ignite a branch.

Kalo was a natural fighter. Her long featherless legs gave her a distinct advantage. She and Coryn advanced together on the two owls who fought wing to wing, making them an easier target. Without speaking, Kalo and Coryn instinctively knew how to vary their moves. They alternated: One blocked while the other attacked. Coryn landed a solid blow to the Great Gray's port wing. The owl screeched in agony but he kept on fighting. The rabbit kept popping up, leaping in arcs, trying to distract the two owls and throw them off in any way. They were fighting close to the ground now and the combat grew more intense. Coryn had to admit, this Great Gray was tough. He was not letting his injured wing distract him but seemed to have grown angrier and more aggressive — and closer. The rabbit leaped up and, in that second, the Great Gray swooped down, caught the rabbit in its talons, and flung him in an arc. Blood spun through the air. Kalo opened her beak and gave a low agonized scream and then took off after the Great Gray. She hurled herself into a downward plunge, a streak of tawny feathers with sparks flying. There was no scream, just a rush of air from the Great Gray's lungs as Kalo skewered him to the tree with the burning tip of the branch. The Great Gray's companion staggered in flight, and Coryn was now backing him against a large boulder. But then, with an insane surge of energy, the Great Horned reached out and tore the branch from Coryn. Suddenly emboldened, he advanced on Coryn.

Coryn reversed his course, backwinging. He and Kalo were without fire or battle claws. Was Kalo strong enough to pull loose the spear with which she had stabbed the Great Gray — if she could even get to it? Would it still be burning? Coryn suddenly remembered the botkin he had swiped from the grog tree. It was a metal one, slotted to let the coals breathe. The chain from which it was suspended was fairly long. It wasn't that different from a fizgig. The Great Horned had Coryn dancing backward. It might look like a defensive move. It had certainly started out that way, but with every second, Coryn was getting closer to the spot where he had left the botkin hanging. The Horned Owl was clumsy with the ignited branch.

He might set himself on fire before touching Coryn. Suddenly, flames erupted all around them. The black spruce flared like a torch. Coryn did not even stop to think and rushed into the tree. There was a screech and a howl of laughter as the Great Gray realized what had happened. He turned on Kalo, who had almost gone yeep when she saw Coryn fly off into the flames.

"You're alone now. So, come, my dear! Time for your scouring. To the great tree!" He rushed at her. But in that same second something whizzed by like a comet from the flaming tree — a spinning ball of flying sparks with a deadly chain attached. Kalo soared up out of the grasp of the Great Horned just before it hit him. Something sailed off into the sparks: a large head, its yellow eyes staring. The Great Horned's body fell to the ground.

"Coryn!" she gasped.

"Kalo!" Coryn swooped up under her and supported her beneath one wing.

"No, I'm fine, Coryn. I'm really fine. We have to go to the rabbit. The rabbit saved my life. . . ." She paused and looked at Coryn. "As you did," she said shyly.

The rabbit was dying. There was a deep rip in his chest. There was a strange whistling sound as if a low wind was blowing through his lungs. He tried to speak. The flames were spreading. They would have to leave soon or be smoked out by the fire. "Look up!" gasped the rabbit. "Look up."

Coryn and Kalo both looked up into the lowest branches of the closest tree that was not yet burning. Sparkling, like a small constellation fallen to Earth, was the glittering design of a spiderweb.

"It's the last design," the rabbit said in a gurgling whisper. A trickle of blood came from his nose. "Easy to read — an orb weaver's web. Remember Coryn? I told you. They're the easiest. The design is coming to me whole — because it is the last, you see. Find moss, not flames. Clad yourself in green, not fire. And fly . . . fly with the green . . . the green . . ." he gasped. "Fly with the Greenowls of Ambala to the tree."

"Don't leave us," Kalo begged.

"Another web reader will come. They always do." He sighed. It was almost a sigh of contentment, and then the mystic rabbit was gone. The heat from the fire was growing intense.

"We have to go now, Coryn. We have to get moss. We must do as the rabbit told us."

"Yes! Fly with the Greenowls of Ambala!"

CHAPTER TWENTY-SEVEN
The Greenowls Are Coming

The night sky was split with song, and the gizzards of those who sang swelled with a fierce new hope.

The path is a ribbon of moonlight across a dusky sea.
The wind sings a song that beckons us
To that great and mighty tree.

We are the Greenowls of Ambala, clad in raiments of moss,
Sprigged with lichens and grasses
Then gilded with silvery frost.

Fair and square we play — for a sporting lot we are.
We ride the boisterous Balefire gusts
And we reach for every star.

As Soren flew with these owls of the Brad, who could doubt they were not as carefree and happy as they sounded? But their mission was a most serious one, a deadly one. For under these cloaks of green, they wore battle claws and carried scimitars crafted by Gwyndor, who had set up a forge in the deep dell of the Brad. Even more deadly than these weapons were the methods of Danyar, which the owls of the Brad had mastered.

Soren prayed that the coded messages that had passed via Hortense to Pelli had been safely delivered and that she and the others back at the tree were ready to carry out their part of the plan. He looked around as they closed in on the Island of Hoole. It seemed that there were a few more Greenowls than when they had left. *Yes*, he thought, *Gwyndor has most likely decided to come with us. Have Streak and Zan come as well?* he wondered as he glanced at two other birds cloaked in moss. But, no, there were no owls who could compare in size to the two eagles.

Indeed, they were not eagles. Under the thin blankets of moss was a Barn Owl and a Burrowing Owl. Coryn and Kalo had found mousefoot moss in Silverveil when they had fled the fire in the Shadow Forest. They had caught sight of the Greenowls as they flew over Cape Glaux, scores of Greenowls, flying to the great tree. They knew they would not be noticed. But now Kalo seemed alarmed as one flew toward them.

"Who's that, Coryn? I'm worried."

Coryn felt a deep tweak in his gizzard. "My uncle, Soren."

"Oh, dear!" Kalo said weakly. Coryn had told her about the Striga, and his own failures as king. It had been one of the most shameful moments of his life, having to tell this story of his pathetic, reprehensible weakness. He made no excuses, however. He just simply said, "I was a weak fool. I do not deserve to be king."

And Kalo had answered, "I don't think one ever deserves to be king. One must earn it and keep on earning it. You began tonight when you saved me. You shall continue, Coryn. I know."

Now as Soren approached Coryn, he hoped he could keep his identity a secret a bit longer. But he was worried.

"That moss does not grow in Ambala," Soren said, flying close to him. "Where do you hail from?"

It's useless, Coryn thought and began to speak. "I hail from the great tree, but I went afoul, dear Uncle. Now I am back. I am a Guardian — a Guardian of Ga'Hoole."

"Coryn, is this really you?" Soren gasped.

"It is I, Uncle. Please let me join this fight tonight not as king but as a Guardian, with Kalo by my side. Kalo from The Barrens who, on orders of the Striga, was to be brought here tonight to be burned. She fights as fearlessly any Guardian."

At that moment another owl came around. Coryn's gizzard lurched as he spied its blue feathers.

"Fear not, Coryn!" the sage said.

"Tengshu, you are here?"

Soren and Tengshu quickly explained how the owl from the Middle Kingdom had flown the River of Wind to find the cursed owl, whom he knew would prove dangerous.

There was no more time to explain. The bonfires on the beaches of the Island of Hoole had been lit. The Balefire Night games were about to begin.

Soren turned to Coryn. "You two follow me. I'll pass the word to the Band."

"You believe me, Soren, don't you? You believe I have changed?"

"I believe that you are the owl you were always meant to be. You were ill. You are well now."

"Sickness cannot always be an excuse. I failed all of you."

"Then don't fail us now. The plan is simple. We play the games for a while. We have learned that there are prisoners who have been brought to the tree, who will be killed. Owls who, like Kalo, had refused to give up their vanities, their families' possessions, and their books. We may be outnumbered. But Doc Finebeak went searching for hire-claws. We hope he found them. Otulissa and Pelli have been secretly training forces within the tree. We must hope for the best."

The island was now less than a league away.

The Greenowls started one of their most boisterous and jolly songs.

We are the Greenowls of Ambala,
Across thermals we scrambala.
To the top with a bounce
We would like to announce
That downdrafts don't faze us
And hardly amaze us.
We catch bonks on the fly
While eating milkberry pie.
Dance a fine little jig
Then alight on a twig.
Oh, we're the jolliest of jollies,
We mossy green owlies.
So, hip-hip-hooray!
Until night fades to day
And Balefire fades to gray.

"And who do you say they are, Field Marshal Cram?" the Striga asked.

"Owls from Ambala. They call themselves Greenowls because for holidays they clad themselves in green. An ancient custom."

"Perfectly harmless, I suppose. No vanities."

"No, sir. No pearls, nothing like that."

"Which reminds me: any luck in apprehending the notorious Trader Mags?"

"No, sir, but we do have her assistant, Bubbles."

"Have you been able to get anything out of her?"

"No, sir. She's as daft as any magpie you could imagine." He paused. "I just have one question, sir. I was wondering if we should worry that any owls here might be, you know, still loyal to the Band?"

"No. I think I have given these owls what they always longed for. A life without distraction of the vanities. A simpler way. It was the children, the young'uns, who really led the way." He looked down from his perch to the Blue Feather Club. Perhaps the Striga did not notice that Bell, who had been his most ardent early member, was shaking and weeping copious tears.

Bell was crying because she realized how wrong she had been about the Striga. Mrs. Plithiver had told them earlier this evening of the lies the Striga had spread about their father, of how he had deceived Coryn to such a point that he had, as Mrs. Plithiver tried to delicately put it, grown so weak in his gizzard that he had fallen ill. She also told the three B's that they would have to be very brave little owls now. They must do some mighty good pretending because the noble owls, the Guardians like their own dear mum, were going to try their best to set things right.

In the new special ceremonies that had been added to Balefire Night, it was the March of the Toys that came first. The youngest of the owlets — hatchlings and fledglings — had lined up with their favorite toys, owli-poppen, which were down-stuffed animals — usually field mice or tiny chipmunks that they often took to their nests when they went to sleep. All to be heaped on a bonfire. Next were the somewhat older owls like the three B's with their favorite things.

"Stop whimpering, Bell," Bash said.

"It's all right. They'll think she's crying over the berry necklace. And that'll be good pretending, like Mrs. P. told us," Blythe said. She herself was clutching a piece of music — not a favorite one, at least.

"Will you two ever forgive me?" Bell swiveled her head first to Bash and then to Blythe. "Will you ever get to sing, Blythe?"

"Hush! If things work out, yes, I'll sing. And yes, we forgive you."

A little owlet ahead of them began to sob as one of the Blue Brigade pried from her a pretty tail clip with sparkly stones that she had clutched in her beak.

"Now, you don't need this!" said the Boreal Owl harshly. "These fancy things are just silly adornments. They will get in the way of your humility."

The ranks of the Blue Brigade had swelled and they were now singing the songs of relinquishment.

And to the flames consign things vain
Give up your prideful ways.
Submission is the path to grace
Where each owl knows its place.
Bless our Striga for his suffering,
For his enduring pain.
Scour our gizzards of the vanities'
Horrible shameful stain.

A-Glaux!

Bell tried to keep her eyes down as she passed the Striga with her necklace. She was tempted to look up and stick her tongue out at him. How had this blue owl fooled her? It didn't help when Bash and Blythe reminded her that he had even gotten to the king's gizzard. It was her gizzard that he had gotten to, and she should have minded it better. It flinched constantly now, racked with shame. Somehow she had to make things better. Prove herself a better owl. "I will." She muttered the words softly. "I will!" Mrs. Plithiver watched her nervously. But Mrs. P. knew that for all her faults Bell had a steely determination, mettle as strong as anything hammered in Bubo's forge.

"You see that little one there?" The Striga leaned over on his perch above the line of owlets and spoke in a low voice to his field marshal.

"Yes, sir."

"She's the daughter of Soren and Pelli. And she's mine now."

The field marshal wasn't exactly sure what the Striga meant, but he nodded. "Yes, I can see that she has an air of perfect humility."

"Well, not quite perfect yet. But she will. Now review with me again the schedule for this evening."

"This is the first of three marches. The second march is the March of the Diamonds, and then the third is the March of Scurrilous Books."

"Ah, I like to call it the 'March of Pride' because these owls have been the most prideful. Their stubbornness in clinging to their books is most un-Glauxly. They put their gizzards and their minds above Glaux. I have chosen a few of those especially prideful owls for the special relinquishment ceremonies." The Striga churred softly.

"Yes, indeed," the field marshal replied.

"They will be perched on their pedestals of books and then ignited. That will be a surprise for these 'Guardians.' A surprise and a lesson. But I feel we must have a break between these marches. So anticipation can build for the grand climax."

"Oh, yes, indeed. The games begin soon. Right after the March of the Toys finishes. Look — they are perching up now — the Greenowls and the others for the first set of colliering games."

A ruddy-feathered Short-eared Owl perched on a high limb next to a tiny Northern Saw-whet. Their expressions were grim. "All right," Ruby said to Martin. "I guess we have to try and make a good show of it during this colliering thing."

"You're darned right, you do!" Bubo flew in and settled beside them. "We are all actors tonight. Remember what Otulissa said. Just a few rounds, then the March of the Diamonds begins."

"First team to participate!" Elvanryb was the game announcer. "In the colliering competition will be the Guardians' team of Ruby, Short-eared, *Asio flammeus*, member of the colliering chaw, trained under the late great Ezylryb."

"Why's he giving our formal species name?" Ruby asked.

"Buying time," Bubo said softly.

"This magnificent owl, known for her short, steep vertical plunge into exploding tree crowns will be teamed with Martin, Northern Saw-whet, *Aegolius acadius*. This tiny bird is distinguished for his precision wing work, as well as his stylish manipulation of collateral drafts created by fire ladders. He is also renowned for his low-level close-to-ground rolling-ember retrievals. Let's give them a big round of applause!"

The other teams from the opposing kingdoms on the mainland were announced. In this event there would be four sets of two-owl teams simultaneously diving into the fires. They would be judged on speed and the number and quality of coals retrieved.

"And flying under the moss cloak of the Greenowls of Ambala we have Braithe, Whiskered Screech, *Otus trichopsis,* known for his crown-leaping, along with his partner, Tintagel."

Pelli was watching from the hollow where she had lined up for March of the Diamonds. Had he said Tintagel? She blinked. *He's here! My dear Soren is here!* Who else would call himself Tintagel, the name of the castle in the book that she and Soren had read from the *Fragmentum? The Legends of King Arthur and His Knights of the Round Table* was their favorite book. Tintagel! Soren was back. He had come to save the great tree! The word was secretly passed beak to ear slit. The Guardians, the true owls of the great tree, were emboldened. Their message had gotten through.

As Ruby flew up from one of her famous short, steep aerial plunges a voice whispered, "What a 'magnificent *Asio flammeus*'!"

"I knew it was you," Ruby whispered back. "Tinky Town or whatever you're calling yourself. No one does that power dive quite like you. So you're back."

"Absolutely!" Soren whispered.

"The action starts with the March of the Diamonds."

Pelli and Otulissa and the owls in the tunnel were ready. Although the "vanities" they carried sparkled, they were not diamonds at all. That were deadly ice weapons.

Elvanryb announced that there would be a break in the games while the judges reviewed the coals retrieved during the colliering competition. "Between these games and the next set we shall have the March of the Diamonds," he said, turning to the Striga and the owls of the Blue Brigade, who were gathered on the reviewing branches of the great tree.

Another dreadful dirge deploring the evil of vanities and the sins of pride began as two columns of owls led by Otulissa and Pelli flew out. Only the points of their glittering ice picks showed, appearing, indeed, like diamonds. Quentin, the quartermaster, had slipped the longer ice blades under the wings of the owls that were marching on the ground, making two tiers of ice-armed owls.

"I can't believe how many of these the owls were hoarding, but they have learned their lesson now!" said Field Marshal Cram.

"Your work has succeeded, Striga," said another owl who wore not one but two blue feathers.

"Mission accomplished!" said a third rather smugly.

And at precisely that moment, Pelli and Otulissa did a midair four-point roll with a turn and tuck and raced toward the viewing branches followed by ten of the finest fliers from the old Strix Struma Strikers. "Eeeeyow!" The Field Marshal saw half his wing hanging limply at his side. Then a cry went up. "It's the Band!"

The Greenowls of Ambala flung off their moss capes. Some wore battle claws, but some flew clawless, and beneath the fiery clamor of the mounting battle was the strange windy din of the Danyar fighters inhaling their breaths of qui. There was a loud smack as Braithe of the Brad, flanked by two owls on either side, smashed into the main viewing perch, dislodging a dozen of the Blue Brigade.

Cries from the Blue Brigade went up to fetch battle claws, fire branches. For in essence, these owls were weaponless, which was exactly what Pelli and Otulissa had counted on. If they could prevent the Blue Brigade and the Striga from gaining access, this would be a battle easily won.

Ruby was in charge of the Flame Squadron and signaled the lighting, and thirty or more owls flew into the Balefire of burning vanities to spark the branches they had hidden in caches around the tree. The nest-maid snakes had already begun to herd the young'uns into the tree and lead them to safety in the old siege tunnel. Bell looked back and saw her mum flying with her ice pick. Her eyes opened in horror. *She might die. It's all my fault!*

She looked around quickly. No one was watching. Certainly not the blind nest-maid snakes. So Bell made a dash to the nearest port in the tree. *I'm coming, Mum,* she thought. *I'll fight beside you.*

Everything was chaos and confusion. The night whizzed with sparks from the huge Balefire and the ignited branches. Ice weapons sparkled high in the canopy of the tree. The curved-edged scimitars, like scallops of a newing moon, slashed through the darkness. An owl fell to the ground. Bell made her way through the melee of smoke, flying ice chips, and sizzling branches. All she had to do was find a weapon of her own. She could handle an ice pick or one of the short blades. There was a burning twig on the ground. She could do something with that. She seized it, spread her wings, and flew off to find her mother. But where had her mother gone? Pelli had been near the viewing perch close to the thick of the battle. But the heaviest fighting seemed to have moved. A cry rose in the night.

"The Great Hollow's been breached!" Bell saw a rush of owls head for the tree. Then a few of the Blue Brigade flew out, fully clawed, the iron talons extended in attack position. She thought she saw Elvanryb fall as she rushed to the scene. She knew she must drop her fire branch before she flew through the opening of the tree. There were no fire weapons in the tree. No owl would ever fight with fire in the tree. But there had never been a battle within the Great Ga'Hoole Tree in its thousand-year history. Bell crouched now in the harp gallery amid the pile of tangled strings and watched. If only there were a pair of battle claws she could get to. She heard a song rise up with a thumping beat. Great Glaux, it must be Twilight! Every young owl knew of these battle chants, but no one had ever actually heard him. But now the chant pounded in Bell's ear slits. She saw the Great Gray prancing in the air in front of two fierce-looking Great Horneds from the Blue Brigade.

> *Talk about vanities, bunch of wet poop!*
> *Twilight's here to give you the scoop!*
> *You dim-witted creeps feathered blue*
> *Don't mess with me, 'cause I am cruel.*
> *I do me a little Breath of Qui*
> *Smash you to smithereens and let it be.*
> *Let it be, you crazy creeps*
> *Gonna bring you down, gonna make you weep*
> *Call for your mama, call for your pop —*
> *Hey, I'm Twilight, cream of the crop!*

"Awesome!" Bell whispered. Her attention was so riveted on Twilight that she had not noticed that another duel was going on very close to her. "Mum!" The Striga and two others were advancing on Pelli. She was slashing at them with an ice scimitar but they had her backed against the perch rail of the harp gallery. There was a splintering sound and fragments spun through the air. Bell buried herself in the tangled grass strings of the harp. What should she do? She peeked out again. Oh, Glaux! Her mum was defenseless. They were closing in on her. She wanted to call for help. Where was her da? Was there no one to help? The tip of something sparkled in the grass strings of the harp. Bell's eyes widened. It was a splinter of ice from one of the ice scimitars. Big enough for her to use. She wrapped a talon around its base. It cut into the tough hide of her talon, but it didn't bleed. She took a deep breath and powered out of the tangle of grass, wielding the small splinter. It was the perfect size. She hurled herself toward the closest owl, a Barred Owl.

Then the Great Hollow spun. She jabbed forward with the splinter. There was a great spurt of blood. The Barred Owl dropped. She heard an anguished screech, "Bell!" She saw her mum fly away. Free! Just as the word free exploded in her head she felt talons closing around her. The ice splinter was wrenched painfully from her grip. She felt something cold against her neck. A silence fell upon the Great Hollow.

"All right." It was the voice of the Striga. Bell couldn't believe it. She had been caught by the Striga. "Everyone drop their weapons or her head comes off."

"No! No!" Bell cried. She felt shame wash through her. Was she saying "No, don't let me die" or "No, don't drop your weapons"? She was not sure. She did not want to die, but she did not want to live. "It's all my fault. It's all my fault," she wailed. She began to hear the clank of weapons dropping, at first one by one, then a large clatter as the rest fell.

"Yes, that is more like it!" said the Striga. A strange sucking sound filled the silence. Bell saw the flames in the large torches that lit the Great Hollow quiver and then extinguish. She felt the Striga's grip tighten and his heart race as he muttered something in Jouzhen. Was she feeling his wings fold in? Was he going yeep?

And then she was twirling through the air. The Striga had forgotten that one weapon could never be dropped — the Breath of Qui!

"After him," someone yelled.

"Are you all right?" Bell blinked. It was another blue owl who was speaking to her. "I had to hit him hard enough to dislodge her." Tengshu turned to Pelli. "But I couldn't do it with full force or I would have killed her."

Pelli scooped Bell into her wings. "Of course you couldn't!" She sobbed. "Of course."

"But he got away, didn't he?" Tengshu asked.

"Don't worry," Soren said, flying up. "He's gone. Most of the rest are dead. A few followed him out. You saved Bell's life."

"And," Pelli added, turning to Bell. "You saved *my* life."

"I did?" Bell blinked.

"You did," Pelli said, and grasped her daughter. "It was a foolish thing, you sneaking away from the other young'uns. It all turned out well. But still, whatever possessed you?"

"It was my fault. All this was my fault," Bell gasped.

"No!" Pelli said staunchly. "Now you listen to me, Bell. None of this was your fault. It is never a young'un's fault. It is grown owls who are to blame. Grown owls who should know better."

Ruby now raced up. "Otulissa is hurt." She gulped and wilfed. Her ruddy feathers lay flat and sleek against her side. She looked so small.

"Where is she?" Soren asked.

"The matrons are tending her down there on the floor of the Great Hollow. She's too injured to move. She's hurt bad, Soren. Real bad."

"Go to her, Soren. Go to her!" Pelli said. "I'll take care of Bell."

CHAPTER TWENTY-EIGHT
A Vigil Is Kept

I'll do what I can do," Fleemus the grizzled Long-eared Owl said. Fleemus was the great tree healer. "But it's a head wound. She's lost a lot of blood, and the eye looks bad. I don't know if I can save the eye." There was a single unspoken thought that passed through the Chaw of Chaws who had gathered around Otulissa, almost a prayer: *For Glaux's sake, save her brain.* What would the tree do without their greatest mind, their greatest ryb. Otulissa, ryb of Ga'Hoolology, scholar of weather interpretation, higher magnetics. The tree without Otulissa's brilliance would be like the tree without the milkberry vines that sparkled in rainbow hues through the twelve cycles of the moon — unthinkable.

Otulissa remained on the floor of the Great Hollow for several nights. She was feverish and often delusional but Fleemus had managed to stop the bleeding and keep any infection at bay. On the fourth night, he said she could be moved to the infirmary. On the sixth night she regained consciousness. And when she woke, she heard Soren and Fleemus and Matron discussing her condition.

"She'll never see out of that port eye," Fleemus was saying. "And infection could still kill her. If I remove the eye, well, she'll be scarred, disfigured, but I think it would lessen the risk of infection."

"Well," Soren said, "if there is one thing that Otulissa isn't, it's vain." He coughed. Even the word sent chills through them.

Otulissa churred silently to herself as she heard them talk. "What makes you so sure I'm not vain, Soren?"

The three owls swiveled their heads around.

"You're awake?" Fleemus asked.

"Awake enough to know that the real question is, can I read with one eye?" She paused. "And who knows, I might be tempted to buy one of those jaunty bandannas from Trader Mags like the one she uses to cover her bald spot. Maybe with some glitter on it. You see, I would like to restore the word 'vanity' to its rightful place in our language. I would like to de-vilify it. Or at least take it out of the realm of the un-Glauxly or whatever that fool owl thought. A little vanity is not a bad thing. I plan to do a linguistical analysis of this word and interpret it in a framework of moral reasoning to explore . . ." Fleemus, Matron, and Soren looked at one another in wonder.

Soren felt his gizzard trembling with joy. *She's back. Brains and all. She's back!*

And she was. Still very weak but gaining strength each night. On warm nights, they moved the brave Spotted Owl to her hanging garden, the one she had tended in the trunk pockets of the tree that even in winter was still lovely with its moon-cycle ferns and huckleberry bushes and snow crocuses. She would often stay there well into the day, for the sun warmed her and made it quite comfortable. She did read, although she tired quickly. So Fritha came often to read aloud to her. They took particular pleasure in reading from the books that they had airlifted to keep safe from the Striga. Kalo, who had settled in the tree with her mate, Grom, her daughter, Siv, son, Bruno, and younger brother, Cory, also came and read to her. Kalo's favorite book was *The Queen's Tale.*

It was a morning late in winter, one of those days that seems to teeter on the cusp of spring, when Kalo was reading to her that Otulissa suddenly interrupted.

"Did I ever tell you, Kalo, about the time I went to the Northern Kingdoms and spent many nights in the great retreat of the Glauxian Brothers? It is located on the island where Hoole's egg was sequestered and he hatched out. . . ." Kalo was enthralled with the Northern Kingdoms.

She couldn't believe that Otulissa had never mentioned this trip to her before.

"You've been there?"

"Oh, yes. I speak fluent Krakish, you know."

"You do?"

"Yes, I had a very . . ." She paused. "A very dear friend there. His name was Cleve. He was a prince, actually." Her single eye twinkled.

"Was?"

"Oh, probably still is. So kind. So gentle," she said wistfully, and adjusted the bandanna over the place where her eye had been. The bandanna was not jeweled, but it was lovely, made from a piece of embroidered silk cloth. Mags had given it to her as a gift.

When Kalo finished reading, she had intended to go back to her hollow but instead turned and flew to see Coryn.

"Coryn? May I speak with you?"

"Kalo, you never have to ask. Please come in."

"Has Otulissa ever mentioned an owl in the Northern Kingdoms named Cleve?"

"Cleve of Firthmore?"

"Yes, that's the one."

"She hasn't mentioned him to me directly, but from the Band I have heard about him — him and Otulissa."

"Him and Otulissa?"

"Yes, Gylfie thinks they were in love, but I guess they had differences."

"Well, maybe those differences aren't so great anymore," Kalo said in a musing tone of voice.

"What are you thinking?"

"I think maybe Otulissa needs something more than what we can give her right now. She is languishing in that garden of hers. Yes, it is lovely, but spring is coming and she needs to get out and fly around a bit. And you know, I think she's a little bit frightened to try flying with one eye. Her wings weren't injured but it's almost as if there is some connection between her missing eye and that wing. She drags it around."

"Yes, I know what you mean. I noticed it, too. What are you suggesting?"

"I think we need to get Cleve. We need to go to the Northern Kingdoms and bring him here to visit an old friend."

Coryn blinked. This was a very good idea. Why, it was only the evening before that he had been looking in the flames of his grate and he had seen something that intrigued him in the fire. He had had strange intimations that there was a reason to go to the Northern Kingdoms. Perhaps not only for Cleve. No, something more sinister.

But the shapes in the flames were vague and fleeting. Still, he would go. And perhaps it was not a good idea to take the Band. He would, of course, tell them his plans but the tree was still recovering from the battle on Balefire Night. It would not do for them all to leave at one time. He could go with Kalo, and perhaps Kalo's mate, Grom.

And so it was decided that he and Kalo and Grom would leave in the next newing of the moon, a few short nights away. Ruby would also accompany them since she had been to the Northern Kingdoms before, but few others would be told, especially not Otulissa. This was to be a surprise.

CHAPTER TWENTY-NINE

An Old Friend

She's up there in the garden. Just fly straight up."
Matron, the burly Short-eared Owl who was head of
the nursing staff, directed.

"Yes, ma'am. I thank you so much!" the Spotted Owl
said. His speech was tinged with the Krakish burr.

He flew around the tree until he came to what was
called the starboard side crotch, where another trunk
branched off from the main one. It was his first visit ever
to the Great Ga'Hoole Tree and he marveled at the array
of subsidiary trunks that split from the main one and
loomed toward the sky like a maze of radiating spires
soaring into the night. The tree was truly as remarkable as
he had heard.

Cleve had been intrigued when he had learned of
the hanging garden that Otulissa had cultivated in the
lower part of the canopy in the soil that collected in
the tree lap.

He paused as he caught sight of her perched on a mossy hump. Her back was to him. He did not want to startle her. She seemed to be studying the stalks of a cladonia, one of the most beautiful lichens.

"Vreeling cladonia mich vaargen, scmuttz engen guneer gunden," Cleve spoke softly.

Otulissa gasped. Her gizzard shuddered. She dared not turn around. Was she dreaming? This could not be true. Someone was speaking to her in beautiful Krakish about the amazing diversity of cladonia lichen. It had been so long since she had heard Krakish spoken.

She slowly turned around. Tears spilled from her one good eye. "Bisshen ninga Krakish y faar son."

"You speak lovely Krakish, Otulissa. I never forgot your voice. I never will."

"Cleve! Cleve!" That was all she could say. Her gizzard quaked with so many emotions that she could hardly speak. *He is still so handsome. How could he ever . . .*

But he had flown right up to her and wrapped her in his wings. "I have missed you, Otulissa."

"But, Cleve, I am so different now."

"You are the same beautiful, smart Spotted Owl that I fell in love with long ago."

She extricated herself from his wings and raised a talon and tore off the bandanna. The pit where her eye had been had healed but the scar was still fresh. "Look at me!"

"What do you take me for, Otulissa? It is the whole owl you are that matters."

"But, Cleve, I got this wound in battle. You are a gizzard-resister. I am a warrior. That is why we parted, remember?"

"I remember."

"Have you changed?"

"No. Have you?"

Otulissa didn't answer but looked down at her talons. What was she to say? She wasn't just a warrior, but she still believed that there were times when force was called for.

"I thought so." Cleve nodded. "You haven't changed and nor have I. But, Otulissa, we are both much more than we were. You are more than a warrior, and I am more than a gizzard-resister. I am a healer now, an herbalist. That was what I was studying at the retreat. You see, we are both more than the sum of our parts. And together..."

I can't believe this is happening, Otulissa thought. But it was. Could she raise young'uns with only one eye? It seemed to her that it took at least a dozen eyes to keep chicks in order. So what difference did one eye more or less make?

*   *   *

In another part of the tree, in the King's hollow, Coryn poked at the fire and watched the flames flare up, then settle down. He bent forward. Once again, he was seeking the rich images between in the central plane. These were the shapes that one with firesight sorted out to make some kind of sense from the images. And these were making a kind of sense, though a dreadful one. Coryn saw another cave, not the one in the canyonlands, but an ice-bright cave, and in it he saw two owls huddled. One cast a blue shadow on the wall of ice. The other raised her face. It loomed like a pitted ice moon. Coryn touched the scar that ran down his own face. It was not his own reflection in the flames. It was Nyra's and, facing her, stood the Striga. His gizzard turned. He was horrified, but at the same instant he felt something stronger and more powerful. For deep in his gizzard, Coryn finally knew that he was free — free from the haunting doubts about his mother, his own blood. *I know at last who I am. And who I am not. I was born of a haggish owl, and though her blood flows through me I am my own owl. My gizzard is mine. I am a king, but more important, I am a Guardian.*

Coryn knew that he needed only courage to make strong the weak, mend the broken, vanquish the proud, and make powerless those who abused the frail. He reached for the first book of the legends, and placed his talon on it. And began to whisper the oath of the Guardians of Ga'Hoole. "I am the eyes in the night, the silence within the wind. I am the talons through the fire, the shield that guards the innocent. . . ." And finally Coryn thought, *I am free, truly free!*

OWLS
and others
from the

GUARDIANS OF GA'HOOLE SERIES

The Band

SOREN: Barn Owl, *Tyto alba*, from the Forest Kingdom of Tyto; escaped from St. Aegolius Academy for Orphaned Owls; a Guardian at the Great Ga'Hoole Tree and close advisor to the King

GYLFIE: Elf Owl, *Micranthene whitneyi*, from the desert kingdom of Kuneer; escaped from St. Aegolius Academy for Orphaned Owls; Soren's best friend; a Guardian at the Great Ga'Hoole Tree and ryb of the navigation chaw

TWILIGHT: Great Gray Owl, *Strix nebulosa*, free flier, orphaned within hours of hatching; Guardian at the Great Ga'Hoole Tree

DIGGER: Burrowing Owl, *Speotyto cunicularius*, from the desert kingdom of Kuneer; lost in desert after attack in which his brother was killed by owls from St. Aegolius; Guardian at the Great Ga'Hoole Tree

The Leaders of the Great Ga'Hoole Tree

CORYN: Barn Owl, *Tyto alba*, the young king of the great tree; son of Nyra, leader of the Pure Ones

EZYLRYB: Whiskered Screech Owl, *Otus trichopsis*, Soren's former mentor, the wise, much-loved, departed ryb at the great Ga'Hoole Tree

Others at the Great Ga'Hoole Tree

OTULISSA: Spotted Owl, *Strix occidentalis*, chief ryb and ryb of Ga'Hoolology and weather chaws; an owl of great learning and prestigious lineage

MARTIN: Northern Saw-whet Owl, *Aegolius acadicus*, member of the Chaw of Chaws; a Guardian at the Great Ga'Hoole Tree

RUBY: Short-eared Owl, *Asio flammeus*, member of the Chaw of Chaws; a Guardian at the Great Ga'Hoole Tree

EGLANTINE: Barn Owl, *Tyto alba*, Soren's younger sister

MADAME PLONK: Snowy Owl, *Nyctea scandiaca*, the elegant singer of the Great Ga'Hoole Tree

MRS. PLITHIVER: blind snake, formerly the nest-maid for Soren's family; now a member of the harp guild at the Great Ga'Hoole Tree

OCTAVIA: Kielian snake, nest-maid for many years for Madame Plonk and Ezylryb (also known as BRIGID)

ELYAN: Great Gray Owl, *Strix nebulosa*, member of the parliament unwholesomely in thrall to the Ember of Hoole

DOC FINEBEAK: Snowy Owl, *Nyctea scandiaca*, famed freelance tracker once in the employ of the Pure Ones

Characters from the Time of the Legends

GRANK: Spotted Owl, *Strix occidentalis*, the first collier; friend to young King H'rath and Queen Siv during their youth; first owl to find the ember

HOOLE: Spotted Owl, *Strix occidentalis*, son of H'rath; retriever of the Ember of Hoole; founder and first king of the great tree

H'RATH: Spotted Owl, *Strix occidentalis*, king of the N'yrthghar, the frigid region known in later times as the Northern Kingdoms; father of Hoole

SIV: Spotted Owl, *Strix occidentalis*, queen of H'rath of the N'yrthghar; mother of Hoole.

KREETH: Female hagsfiend with strong powers of nacht-magen; friend of Ygryk, conjures Lutta into being

Other Characters

DUNLEAVY MACHEATH: treacherous dire wolf, once leader of the MacHeath clan in Beyond the Beyond

GYLLBANE: courageous member of the MacHeath clan of dire wolves; her pup Cody was maimed by clan leader Dunleavy MacHeath

BESS: Boreal Owl, *Aegolius funerus*, daughter of Grimble, a guard at St. Aegolius Academy for Orphaned Owls; keeper of the Palace of Mists (also known as THE KNOWER)

BRAITHE: Whiskered Screech Owl, *Otus trichopsis*, owl from Ambala and a memorizer of books; flew with the Greenowls of Ambala to the great tree on Balefire Night

Blue Owls

STRIGA: Blue Snowy Owl, *Nyctea scandiaca*, a former dragon owl from the Middle Kingdom seeking a more meaningful life (also known as ORLANDO)

TENGSHU: Blue Long-Eared Owl, *Asio otis*, qui master and sage of the Middle Kingdom

A peek at

THE GUARDIANS *of* GA'HOOLE
Book Fifteen: *The War of the Ember*

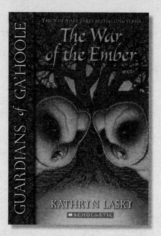

"All right," Ruby said, taking a step closer to the others. "You've studied the charts. You each know your individual flight plan."

"Yes," Fritha answered. "I am to go due east from here into the canyonlands, then circle back west and head for Beyond the Beyond, and head straight out toward the Wolf's Fang."

"And you, Wensel?"

"Yes ma'am." Wensel then repeated the details of his route.

"Excellent!" Bess replied after they had recited their individual flight plans. She accompanied them to the turret opposite the bell tower and watched them take off into the wildness of the storm. She had to wedge herself into one of the stone turret notches to keep from being swept off. The raging wind blew the cascading water of the falls in horizontal sheets across the night. Trees shuddered, the noise of their branches a drumbeat beneath the wind. Flashes of lightning illuminated the undersides of rolling clouds, giving them a harsh metallic glow, and always that odd whining that sliced through the wind's roar, splitting it like a talon through tender flesh.

But the three owls were amazing fliers. Bess watched as they lifted off into the teeth of the storm. Catching every favorable draft, they manipulated their wings constantly to adjust to the confusing air currents. There were alarming shifts and abrupt shears where a wind could accelerate or decelerate dramatically, change its direction completely, pocking the air with deadfalls and suck-down vents, which could spell disaster for the average flier. But these were no average fliers. "Glaux speed," she murmured softly as she saw them dissolve into a thick dark cloud bank. "Glaux speed!"

Out past the reach
of the Ga'Hoole Tree,
where survival is the
only law, live the
Wolves of the Beyond.

New from Kathryn Lasky

WOLVES OF THE BEYOND

In the harsh wilderness beyond
Ga'Hoole, a wolf mother hides in
fear. Her newborn pup has a twisted
paw. The mother knows the rigid
rules of her kind. The pack cannot
have weakness. Her pup must be
abandoned—condemned to die. But
the pup, Faolan, does the unthinkable.
He survives. This is his story—the story
of a wolf pup who rises up to change
forever the Wolves of the Beyond.

■ SCHOLASTIC
www.scholastic.com